Judy Cornwell was born in London and ~~~~~~
Australia and Sussex. She is one of Britain's leading actresses, whose stage career spans the Joan Littlewood Theatre Workshop, the RSC, the West End and the acclaimed 1993 national tour of *The Cemetary Club*. Her most recent international film was *Santa Claus – The Movie*. Her countless TV performances include the phenomenally successful BBC comedy series, 'Keeping Up Appearances'. *Fear and Favour* is her fourth novel, following *Cow and Cow Parsley*, *Fishcakes at the Ritz*, and *The Seventh Sunrise*.

Judy Cornwell is married to the broadcaster and journalist, John Parry. They have one son, Edward, and live in Brighton.

Also by Judy Cornwell

Cow and Cow Parsley
Fishcakes at the Ritz
The Seventh Sunrise

FEAR
AND
FAVOUR

Judy Cornwell

SIMON & SCHUSTER

LONDON · SYDNEY · NEW YORK · TOKYO · SINGAPORE · TORONTO

First published in Great Britain by Simon & Schuster Ltd, 1996
First published in Pocket Books, 1996
An imprint of Simon & Schuster Ltd
A Viacom Company

Simon & Schuster Ltd
West Garden Place
Kendal Street
London W2 2AQ

Simon & Schuster of Australia Pty Ltd
Sydney

A CIP catalogue record for this book is available
from the British Library

ISBN 0-671-85362-7

Typeset in Sabon 11/13.5pt by
Palimpsest Book Production Limited, Polmont, Stirlingshire
Printed and bound in Great Britain by
Caledonian International Book Manufacturing Ltd,
Glasgow

This book is dedicated to my dear friend
Suzanne Lucas

1

The morning after the hurricane of 1987, he had walked down West Street, the road leading up from the seafront to the Clock Tower, in the centre of the town. People were walking about in a distressed, dazed condition. Buildings were smashed, trees torn up by the roots, and the wind howled angrily round every corner, into every lane and passageway.

While pushing against the buffeting wind, he was watching great, grey, furious waves heaving against the promenade, when he saw it. It was upside down, embedded in the pavement. An icy gust of wind whipped his priest's collar then pressed cold fear down his spine. It was the crucifix from the spire of Saint Paul's Church.

It was as if Old Nick had started the chaos in the town then, eight years ago, Father Peter thought. He sat in the restricted twilight of the confessional, allowing time to pass before the next penitent brought a new rhythm to his heartbeat, and mulled over the pattern of events that had happened in the town since the hurricane.

He had prayed daily for understanding, for the answers to why so many terrible things had happened. Anger hung like a heavy, static shroud over Brighton. He had felt it acutely last November, on the Feast of Andrew the Apostle, to be exact. He had been walking along the elm-tree-lined street towards Saint Mary Magdalene's when he had heard what

1

sounded like the rushing of a thousand malignant spirits. He had turned in fear, a prayer already formed on his lips, only to see that the trees had shed their leaves in one great fall, becoming naked, grey, skeletal shapes in the eerie yellow of the streetlamps.

Since then he had seen the fear of hope in the eyes of the homeless, sleeping rough in shop doorways, the fear of faith in the faces of the young, schooled in the eighties philosophy of survival of the fittest, and heard fear of charity in the harsh street sounds where mindless violence turned every unexpected noise into an imminent threat. He woke each night to Old Nick's discordant symphony of wailing police sirens, aggressive, drunken, angry howls and loveless children's vicious swearing.

The beastliness of mankind roamed the town.

'It's no different to anywhere else, Father,' Mike O'Reilly had assured him, as he had laid out the weekly newsletter. 'If I hear footsteps behind me these days, I stop and let whoever it is pass. I pretend to blow my nose or do up a button, anything so I can take a look out of the corner of my eye, you see.'

Mike was a reformed alcoholic who devoted a great part of his life to helping around the church. He was an ex-sailor who had been treated in a naval hospital before returning to his home town and settling down. He lived simply in a rented furnished flat close to the church, supplementing his pension by the occasional painting and decorating work and odd gardening jobs, and, in the warmer weather, by helping some of the fishermen who operated from the Marina. He had brought many friends from Alcoholics Anonymous to the church when they had needed to talk about their past misdeeds. A few stayed on and regularly attended mass, but most of them just wanted to confess once to a priest in confidence, knowing that never, ever, would he betray their secrets.

Father Peter found their honesty and sincerity refreshing, and often found himself turning to Mike when irritated by the day-to-day problems in the church. The old sailor often calmed him when his own temper was roused.

He had contemplated on anger this morning while he was shaving and watching the dark purple sky become streaked by a livid, fiery crimson.

'Red sky in the morning is the shepherd's warning,' his mother used to say in her soft, Norfolk lilt.

He had remembered her voice at dawn, when the radio announcer had warned that the south coast would experience bitterly cold weather. But until noon the harshly bright February sun had still been warming the snowdrops and crocuses in his small walled garden. By three o'clock the clouds had appeared and the weather forecast proved to be true. His knees had begun to twinge as a raw arctic wind brought thick swirling snow, which by dusk, lay in huge luminous drifts against the church walls.

Outside the entrance to Saint Mary Magdalene's, where Mike O'Reilly had salted and swept the pavement earlier, there now lay a thin layer of ice, the cause of all the oaths and blasphemy he could hear as the devout or hardier members of the faith crossed the threshold.

Father Peter stretched his spine. There was nothing like a stiff neck to guarantee instant humility, he mused. His once great battle with lust had now been reduced to a daily quarrel with his limbs. He looked at his watch. Another thirty minutes before he had to prepare for the eight o'clock Saturday mass.

It was while he was hearing Mrs Mahone's confession that he heard the unfamiliar, heavy footsteps. The stranger walked across the back of the church, paused a while, and then returned to sit by the entrance.

There was something familiar about the sound of those footsteps, he thought. Soldier's boots. Of course they were soldier's boots. He should have recognised the heavy tread from his own war years in the marines. Was the stranger some poor troubled soul, fighting the scream of his conscience, he wondered – or just someone seeking refuge from the cold?

Mrs Mahone had enjoyed the same confession for the last twenty years. He had lost count of the number of times he had given her absolution. He knew every detail of her one adulterous affair, relived with squirming pleasure every Saturday. She was now whispering her Hail Marys and Glory Be to the Fathers in the front pew.

He remembered the letter entrusted to him years ago. It contained the confession of another adulterous affair. He should have handed it over long before now but something, some instinct, caused him to withhold it. Although he had reached the age of seventy, he was not quite ready for Saint Peter's pearly gates, not yet, and there were some important questions to be answered. He still felt that the Boss would reveal them, at the right time. His faith in the Boss had never wavered. Not since he was twelve years old and had confronted Him among the cold windswept dunes on the Norfolk coast. He had screamed his childish obscenities across the wet sands, howled with rage that He had taken his beautiful mother away. He had left the beach with the Boss, and Faith.

He wondered how much time he still had left to follow the paths of mysteries. As an optimist, he still hoped for the spirit of youth to return, to take him by the hand, and lead him back to the great anticipation of a new day. A day when he wouldn't be irritated by news presenters who missed out consonants, or whined out the world's dramas in that hideous, mesmerising, singsong way that so repelled him that he lost the thread of whatever story was on offer. He did not want to give in to old age, or to become part of what he saw as the general decline into trivialising mediocrity of everything he believed to be the traditional way of life, but neither did he wish to be an old one, so desperate for peace, that he would accept space and time in a day as only a series of interruptions between meals and fond memories.

A freezing, niggling draught crept under the door of the confessional, reminding him yet again of his own mortality. He was now susceptible to any damp or cold weather. The aches and twinges in his bones were more reliable than any barometer. The old priest tucked his robe round his ankles and blessed the inventor of long johns.

He wondered whether the hesitant stranger needed confession. The old priest waited patiently, straining his ears for sounds of the stranger's approaching steps. It became too difficult. His hearing was confused by the noise of shuffling movements in the pews, the whispering penances and the low moaning wind in the rafters.

The stranger sat waiting at the back of the church until Father Peter emerged from the confessional. Then, after a word from Mike O'Reilly, he stood up, staring intently in the old priest's direction.

Father Peter smiled. His ears had not deceived him. The stranger was a young soldier. Father Peter guessed his age to be about twenty-five. As he came forward to greet him the soldier dropped his intense gaze and stood uneasily, shifting his feet and glancing anxiously towards the entrance, as if being seen speaking to a priest was to invite the presumption of indecency.

'Welcome to Saint Mary Magdalene's,' Father Peter said.

'I'm not a catholic.'

The words were said defiantly. The soldier's eyes had the same haunted, defensive expression that Father Peter remembered seeing on the faces of his battle-fatigued comrades in 1943. The corners of the young man's mouth dimpled downwards. The old priest suspected it was from nervously grinding his teeth. Also, his cheeks were flushing a bright scarlet. Father Peter was not sure whether it was from anger or shyness.

Out of the corner of his eye, he could see Mike O'Reilly rearranging the prayer books. He sensed that Mike was concerned for his safety. He felt apprehensive himself. He knew this stranger could be part of the army of dangerously deranged who were to be found prowling the streets of Brighton – the pitiful failures of the government's ill-conceived community care programme.

'Are you Father Peter?'

'Yes I am,' the priest replied. 'Are you from round here?'

'No.' The soldier handed over a filthy brown paper parcel. 'I was asked by someone to give you this. He wanted me to give it to you in person.'

Father Peter cautiously accepted the package. 'Who was it?'

'I don't know – just a bloke who knew I was coming home to Brighton.'

'Do you know what it is or why the fellow sent it?'

'No idea. I was just asked to give it to you.'

The young man grew restless, irritated by the questions.

'Have you just come back from Northern Ireland?'

'No, Bosnia.'

Father Peter was bewildered. Why should anyone in Bosnia send him a parcel? 'I don't think I know anyone in Bosnia,' he said. 'Were you there long?'

'Too long.'

The soldier bit his lip, then turned suddenly and walked out into the night.

'He was in a bit of a hurry,' Mike said.

Father Peter felt the sweat of fear break out all over his body. Was it a bomb? That would be a good reason to leave so quickly. Perhaps it was ready to explode. If so, he had to get it outside quickly and far away from the church and the congregation.

Heart beating loudly, in time with the imaginary mechanism, and holding the parcel gingerly, the old priest headed towards the entrance. As he walked he squeezed the parcel gently. It might not be a bomb. Explosives need not weigh as much as this did. It was quite solid. Perhaps he was over-reacting. Still, one couldn't be too cautious.

Chest wheezing, his feet slipping and sliding along the pavement, he reached a lamppost and leaned against it. The sweat on his brow and scalp was turning cold and he felt absolutely wretched.

The parcel was tied loosely but he had to force his cold aching fingers to undo the knots in the string. Perhaps it was, after all, just a proper parcel. 'Hail Mary, full of grace, the Lord is with thee . . .' he muttered. The string fell to the snow-covered pavement. 'Blessed art thou among women . . .' Gasping for breath, he peeled back some of the paper. He thought he could see black leather. Was it a book of some sort? Feeling bolder he removed the paper completely. It was a Filofax. Why on earth should someone in Bosnia send him a Filofax?

He turned it over. The tattered piece of paper stuck on the front of the book informed any 'finder' that the Filofax belonged to 'M/s Elizabeth M. Baker, 12, Balfour Lane, Brighton, East Sussex, BN1 6QR. Blood Group O. Donor . . .'

It was Bessie's Filofax.

While it was not a bomb, the impact of what the parcel contained caused an explosion in his mind. The shock brought immediate dizziness. The gurgling rasp he could hear was the noise of his own laboured breathing, as his heart kicked against the walls of his chest.

He held on to the streetlamp and forced his lungs to monitor the panic. After about five minutes of insane imagery, which slowly dispersed after he had repeated seven intensely focused Hail Marys, his breathing regained normality and he was able to face the reality of his situation.

He was in possession of a stolen book. It had been missing since 1990 and should be handed over to the police.

The theft of this Filofax had been the beginning of a time of fear. The fear had become panic and ended in three murders. The three victims had three things in common. They were all Justices of the Peace, they were all catholics, and they were all members of his congregation.

Father Peter knew that any journalist would turn cartwheels if given this book. Not since the 1984 IRA bomb explosion at the Grand Hotel had the national press focused so much attention on Brighton. And not since the police corruption trials of the late fifties had those involved with law enforcement been subject to so much scrutiny.

There had always been features about the town in the national papers. Journalists complained about its sleaziness, the overpriced hotels and rundown appearance. The town was supposed to be a microcosm of the metropolis. It was known as London by the Sea. Placards in Dr Brighton's, a famous seafront pub, informed the drinker that, 'When you're tired of Brighton, you're tired of life.'

In 1990 writers had said the sleaze and signs of recession in the old seaside town were merely reflections of the sleaze and recession in Britain. Then the journalists began writing features about the whole judicial system. Were the justices selected suitable people? The victims' lives were scrutinised and speculated about. This was followed by articles critical of a cheap legal system based on misplaced values. Disillusioned magistrates fuelled the debate by writing to different papers complaining about changes in the courts, and saying that, in an age of marketplace philosophy, society should appreciate them for giving their services for nothing.

Tucking the Filofax carefully under the folds of his robe,

the priest walked slowly back to the church, wondering why he had been given this book? Was it the Boss, moving in His mysterious way, to grant an old priest the favour of answering questions that had haunted him for years? Was it possible that it could identify the murderer? And would he now begin to understand the anger?

Father Peter stared at the Filofax. He now regretted having left the message for Stella. The poor woman had been nearly mad with grief when Bessie's body was found. Bessie had been like a second mother to her.

'I have no one now, Father,' Stella had sobbed, 'No one of my own.'

Why he had telephoned so late he couldn't think. Panic probably. He felt he had to tell someone and Stella was the first to come to mind. She was due back in England any day now. Through the south-facing window he could see the snow still gently falling on to the roofs and becoming quite deep in the school playground below.

He hadn't told Mike, who had looked at him with obvious curiosity when he returned to the church to get ready for the eight o'clock mass. He'd forced a laugh and said, 'Not a bomb, just a book I'd lent someone.' He knew his face had flushed red with the lie, and felt sadness that Mike had sensed his dishonesty. After mass, having consumed the supper prepared by Mrs Huggins – and praised her profusely, as he did every mealtime – he escaped upstairs and prepared himself to open Bessie's diary.

Why did he feel so apprehensive? Was it the thought of confronting his own past sins? Or reliving the terrible lust that overcame him that summer? He suddenly felt very tired and old. Could it be the lack of commitment to a task given by the Boss – something for which he'd prayed for the last five years?

9

'Oh Lord, tell me why. Please tell me why there has been such violence. Oh Lord let your servant understand.'

He had forgotten the golden rule he always taught the children: 'Be careful what you pray for, because sometimes you are given it and it may not be what you really want.'

'Oh come on man,' he muttered fiercely to himself, 'let's have a little honesty please. You don't want to open this diary because you're just afraid. Fear again. That's what has made you reach out selfishly. You're an old soldier feeling your age, about to go into battle. And you're scared you don't have the strength or the intellect to complete the mission. You want Stella to share the responsibility.'

He groaned with the self-confrontation. So many secrets, so many lies, twists and knots to unravel.

He had once gone on a pilgrimage to Santiago de Compostela. It was the summer of 1975. On the journey he had met up with a Jesuit, David, who was about to be sent to Ethiopia. They decided to travel together and the fortnight spent in the other man's company was one of the happiest times Father Peter had ever known. They had never met again, but the memory of the conversations was as clear as if they'd taken place yesterday.

'It takes genius to simplify,' David once said, when they were discussing the mysteries over supper. 'At the beginning of a mystery, I find I have to throw away all logic and turn the questions over to my inner self, or intuition. I find, after I get an answer, I can then ruthlessly apply my faculties of reason. When I reach the point of my reason's limitation, I then get a glimmer of reality and understanding.'

'So be it,' Father Peter now whispered, as he drew the curtains, blocking out the draughts, found a biro and a notebook, pulled a chair up to his desk and opened the Filofax.

Resting inside was the small Magistrates' Year Book for 1990. Father Peter frowned. It was the loss of this little book that had caused the initial fear and panic.

He turned to the index page and found a list consisting of the chairman, followed by the names of five deputy chairmen, the Juvenile Panel chairman, the Domestic Panel chairman, then the name of the Clerk to the Justices, the Deputy Clerk to the Justices, and a list of court clerks. Bessie Baker and Charles Nightingale were both deputy chairmen.

Father Peter turned the page to find the names and addresses of all the Justices in order of seniority. The dates when they joined the bench were in the left-hand column beside their names. Bessie's was the fifth name down the list: '1975 – Baker, Miss Elizabeth Mary.' Underneath hers was, '1975 – Nightingale, Mr Charles Gordon.'

Father Peter had not realised that Bessie and Charles had joined in the same year. What a coincidence, he thought. He had met them both in the same year too. He had met them in 1952, when he was twenty-seven and had just arrived at the red-brick Saint Mary Magdalene's with its elaborately carved stone dressings and tall spire. He had felt rather disgruntled that he had been sent to Brighton, Sussex, rather than somewhere more exciting. He'd wanted to go to Africa or South America as some of his friends had.

'Did you know Sussex was the last county to become Christian?' he told the old retiring priest, Father John, after reading an old book on the area.

'Oh,' the old man replied. 'And when did that happen?'

Father John had introduced him to Bessie. She had arrived breathless and excited at the sacristy to tell Father John about her new job as a railway booking clerk with Southern Region. When they shook hands Bessie had blushed. She was nearly twenty-two, dressed very neatly in a navy pleated skirt and crisp white blouse, and was wearing her fair hair in a pageboy style. He thought she looked very pretty, a bit like June Allison. After giving Father John all the details of her work, she turned and ran back up the hill to the row of shabby terraced houses where she lived.

'Now that young woman should be an inspiration to you, Peter,' Father John said to him. 'Her mother died when she was only fourteen, so she left school and ran the home for her father, and helped bring up her four younger brothers and sisters. Ron Baker is a train-driver, a good man. He works hard but those flats up there are depressing places. You'll be visiting a few soon. Reminds me of some parts of Dublin. Rows of grand old buildings with black ironwork balconies, all gone to seed.

'Anyway, as I was saying, that little girl, Bessie, kept the place as clean as a pin. Not one of those younger children ever had a button off, and they were always on time for mass. She got her pocket money by cleaning a couple of mornings a week in some of the grander houses down the hill from her place. And you know, Peter, it's only now, now that little Dawn is well settled in school, that it's possible for that lovely Bessie to be able to take a proper job. And she's a good brain on her. She'll probably get quick promotion, you'll see.'

Father John's faith in Bessie's ability proved to be correct, Father Peter thought. When she retired in 1990 she had reached the position of personnel manager at Brighton Station. Her brothers and sisters all turned out to be a credit to her, too. The eldest brother, John, was a bank manager in Canada. The younger boy, Mark, was now a teacher in a Bognor college. The two girls became nurses in New Zealand, then married, and now had families of their own. Bessie had always been proud of their achievements.

A week after their first meeting in 1952, he did knock on the dingy door of her flat. She was living in Saint Michael's Place. A poor, shabby street in those days, of four-storey terraced housing built in the late 1860s with angular bays and black, rusting ironwork balconies. It was about two hundred yards uphill from Saint Mary Magdalene's, and at noon lay in the shadow of the Gothic-style, red-brick church of St Michael and All Angels. He wanted to talk to her about her sister Jean's confirmation.

She wasn't in but someone emerged from the next flat. That was his first meeting with Tadeusz and Halina Potocki. As soon as she saw his priest's collar, Halina invited him in. They were Polish refugees. They had been among the thousands of Poles deported to Russia in 1939. Then, when Germany invaded Russia, Tadeusz had been part of the quickly formed Polish army, taken over by the British, and sent to Persia for training. His wife had been shipped with some of the other soldiers' families through the Caspian Sea and across to India, where they had waited in camps until the end of the war.

Tadeusz had fought in North Africa and then taken part in the famous battle of Monte Cassino. When the war was over he was among the thousands of Poles who chose to come to Britain. Halina couldn't join him until 1948.

They had both slaved in London hotel kitchens trying to save up enough money to start a business. In 1952, when he met them, they had just moved into the flat, having acquired the lease of a small restaurant close to the Hippodrome Theatre. Tadeusz told him they had chosen Brighton because of the large Polish community there.

While Tadeusz went into the shabby kitchen to get him some beer, Halina whispered, 'Fahder, I tink I am having baby. You are first person I tell. Maybe is lucky for me, to tell priest. Will you bless me Fahder?' Later that year, at the end of October, he had baptised their baby daughter, Stella.

Tad was not built to wear suits. He had squeezed himself into a cheap one for the occasion and spent the entire ceremony in stoic discomfort, pulling at the suit sleeves at every opportunity.

Quiet, timid Halina had held the sturdy baby with an

expression of wonder Father Peter would never forget, as if she could not understand how her own fragile body had produced such a child. She wore a dowdy ill-fitting dress which emphasised her painful thinness. All the money had been spent on Stella's christening robe, which was made of layer upon layer of Irish lace. What wheeling and dealing Tad had done to get the lace Father Peter could only guess.

Two weeks later, in November, he baptised Maureen Parker, who was born in the same block of flats as Stella. Her christening robe was well laundered but had been worn on five previous occasions and some of the lace was in need of repair. Maureen was the sixth child of Robert Parker, a well-educated man who had been a prisoner of war in a Japanese concentration camp. Because of his experiences there, he was unable to work, and he lived on a very meagre pension.

Luckily, Betty, his wife, was a trained nurse. The money she earned from her part-time work supplemented their income. But they were poor. The children were intelligent and well behaved but always shabby. Their clothes were passed down from child to child. Pockets were added to cover worn material on the girls' skirts and patches were sewn on to the elbows of the boys' jumpers and blazers.

The Parkers' flat was always clean and tidy, just like Bessie's, and on every shelf or table there were always piles of library books.

Early in December 1952, he baptised Jenny Rutter, the child the angels had granted every favour. Her home had been one of the large semi-detached villas in a wide tree-lined street running downhill from the poorer area. Once it was a bluebell wood and every spring the front garden of each villa was scattered with clumps of the flowers. Jenny was an only child, born to rich, doting parents, and her baptism was an unusually elegant, well-dressed event, in a church used

14

to people coping for so long with clothes rationing. Jenny's christening gown was from Harrods, and it was made of the finest lace. Seedpearls had been sewn in patterns over the gown. Even as a tiny infant Jenny had looked like a beautiful princess.

At another well-heeled affair that same week, Charles Nightingale, a bright, good-looking, young national service-man on weekend leave, came with an American friend to attend a wedding service. A young Italian boy, the son of a London ceramics dealer, was marrying a local girl.

It had been Charles's first visit to Brighton. Father Peter remembered him being anxious to get out of army life and into the world of leisure. He was very much a young man in a hurry, he remembered thinking, ambitious and keen to prove to his parents that he could make his own way in the world without having to go into the family fish business. His American friend had sold him on the idea of slot machines as the way to future easy money.

Father Peter had watched him dancing and been slightly disturbed by the way he treated the young women at the party. There was a hard edge to him, which the priest suspected was a fear of feeling emotion. As the wine took hold later, Charles had confided in Peter how he had just been dumped by his girlfriend. The priest had felt sad for him, knowing that he, like so many vulnerable people, had taken the decision that he would never allow himself to be hurt again. He turned his attention back to the names on the Justices list: '1981 – Evans, Prof Maureen Ann.'

Maureen had been the last one to leave Saint Michael's Place. Tad and Halina had left in the late fifties to live over the new restaurant they had bought in the Lanes. In the mid sixties, just before Halina died, they moved to a large house with grounds on the outskirts of Brighton. Bessie moved out in the late seventies but Maureen's parents never left. Betty Parker died a few months after Maureen left for Oxford in the early seventies and Robert Parker died later the same year. Although she sometimes visited her older sisters during the holidays, Maureen had not returned to Brighton until the early eighties, when she was offered a post at Sussex University and the opportunity of buying Jenny's old house.

While she was at Oxford she had met and married a theatre director, Jack Evans. They had two children, a boy and a girl, and when Maureen moved into Jenny's old house it was like a dream fulfilled. She had always loved the street. Father Peter remembered her when she was a child, sobbing in confession after attending Jenny's seventh birthday party.

'I've coveted Jenny's house, Father, and I burst her balloon on purpose.'

He remembered how difficult it was to be serious as he asked, 'And why did you burst Jenny's balloon?'

'Because she's got everything,' came the wailed reply.

It was in the late sixties, when Maureen must have been about fifteen years old, that Father Peter realised how seriously she felt about Jenny's house. It was during one fine autumn night while he was taking a leisurely stroll up the street that he saw a car full of young people pull up outside the Rutters' home. Maureen got out, let herself in through the gate, then turned and waved goodbye. As soon as she was sure the others were out of sight, she ran up the hill to her own place. Father Peter sighed and turned the page of the Justices list: '1983 – Allan, Jennifer Sian.'

His mouth puckered involuntarily and he felt a great heaviness in his heart. Jenny, his favourite child, and, next to his mother, the person he believed to be the most beautiful woman in the world. As a small child she had looked like an angel with her blonde curly hair, her round innocent blue eyes and her smiling, sunny nature. It was natural to cast her as the Angel Gabriel in the school nativity play. She had loved standing on the rostrum, her silver wings taking up a good part of the small stage so that the shepherds, three rather self-conscious boys, were squeezed down into the footlights. Maureen had been the Virgin Mary and Stella had been the narrator.

The three little girls had been inseparable, plotting mischief one minute, rowing the next. Father Peter would watch them with pride while they ran round the school playground. They were his first three baptised ones.

After finishing primary school, the three girls had all attended the local convent. Then, when Maureen and Stella left for their respective universities, Jenny was sent to a finishing school in Switzerland. During her time there, her parents sold the Brighton home and retired to the South of France.

When she left the school in Switzerland, Jenny played the international scene for a few years before eventually marrying a rich young Sussex farmer, Robert Allan. When she returned to Sussex to be married at Saint Mary Magdalene's, Father Peter was overjoyed. She was the most beautiful bride he had ever seen.

The couple lived in a wonderful old manor house about fifteen miles from Brighton. Father Peter was often asked to parties there, and to the occasional summer party thrown on *Jester*, their motor yacht, which was moored in the Brighton Marina.

When Father Peter told Jenny that Maureen had bought her old home, she had been thrilled that she would be able to visit it again.

He looked at his watch. Almost midnight and he had to be up early in the morning. He turned another page: '1986 – Potocki, Stella Maria.'

He remembered going with Bessie, Maureen and Jenny to see Stella sworn in. Afterwards they had all had lunch together at Maureen's. Those were the happy days, when all his girls were with him. Mike O'Reilly used to laugh and say, 'Here come Father Peter's girls.' There was so much laughter and life. Bessie, Stella, Maureen and Jenny gave so much of their time to the church.

Next to the Magistrates' Year Book, staring straight at him, was a picture of Saint Jude, the patron saint of hopeless cases, as old Father John used to say. Father Peter made a mental note to offer up a prayer to Saint Jude tonight before he went to sleep.

In the diary section of the Filofax, there was a space of about two inches per day, three days a page, with an extra space at the bottom for notes.

Sunday, 31st December 1989 (New Year's Eve)
Take trifle. Stella picking me up at 7pm.

Then in the small space for notes at the bottom of that page:

New Year resolutions – 1, Try to be more positive in the retiring room, not so cynical about the way the courts are disintegrating.

2, If not elected Chairman of the Bench, leave and go to New Zealand and see Dawn and Jean. Must be here next year in case he tries to contact me. I hope he will.

To read a woman's diary was such an intimate experience. Seeing all the personal details of Bessie's life reminded him of when he used to go into his mother's bedroom as a child. He would step into a feminine sanctum of coloured potions, sweet-smelling jumbles of soft things to touch, and would trace the flowered patterns on her frocks.

Bessie's writing was extremely neat. He picked out what he thought were possibly relevant jottings and copied them into his notebook.

Wednesday, 3rd January
   6pm – see Mike O'Reilly for kitchen estimate.

He remembered Mike joking about the new tiles he was
fitting for her. 'I've got to copy one of these magazine
pictures she likes, Father. It's all going to be shades of
white. Even the floor is going to be white tiled. I said to
Miss Baker, I said don't get ill or no one'll find you.'

Thursday, 4th
   NG Shoplifting all day. Claim lunch allowance.
Friday, 5th
   *They did me proud at my retirement party. Had a
good cry.*

Thursday, 11th
   Old Sam up on drunk charge.

Father Peter took note. Old Sam was Mike's friend. They
had been in the navy together.

Monday, 15th
   *Sam and Mike coming round for talk. Mike starting
next Monday 22nd, on kitchen.*
   Friday, 26th
   *Alternative to Custody training session. Licensing talk
7.30pm to 9.10. Counts as 1 hour's training.*
   Monday, Feb 12th
   *4.30. Bail Information scheme. Very worried about
Maureen. It looks as if she may lose the house. Have
advised her not to sit on cases where she may be
prejudiced. Stella's Dinner party. Take Banoffi pie.*

Father Peter remembered Maureen and Jack being in

19

financial trouble. It had been caused by the hurricane of 1987. A large chimney pot had been blown through the roof and just missed killing one of their children by a few feet. Maureen had sworn it was a miracle that the child had been spared. But then they ran into problems with the insurance company. It involved taking the company to court. They had obviously resolved their problems, Father Peter decided, because they were still in their house. He looked back at the diary.

Tuesday, 27th March
Jenny back from Barbados, the blouse undone just a little too far for court. Is she making a play for CN? Moaning about learning the new security number. She announced to the entire retiring room that she was going to change her PIN numbers and her safe combination numbers to the court security number. She didn't hear the sarcasm when someone said, 'How many safes do you have?' Stupid woman replied, 'Two, one on Jester and the other at the farm.' She really does not understand. It's always the same when she returns from mixing with the rich abroad.

Father Peter frowned. It was unlike Bessie ever to say unpleasant things about anyone, and he felt deeply disappointed that she should write in such a disparaging way about Jenny. He sighed and continued to read the diary.

Tuesday, 17th April
Sam coming round at 7pm.
Monday, April 23rd
Sam did phone. sober. going out May 2nd. He will wait by groyne at 9pm. Check Hastings and Min of Agriculture and Fisheries.
Friday, 27th April
Criminal Justice Act. Concerned about the way BR is

going. How will people travel long distances on one ticket
if all the regions are with different private companies?
Wednesday, 2nd May
*Hope Sam turns up & it's not a waste of everyone's
time.*
Tuesday, 8th May
Sam not phoned in.
Wednesday, 9th May
S's body found drowned, or was he murdered?
Monday, 14th May
*See Mike O'Reilly at the crematorium. Stella booked
with dentist so Jenny says she'll drive me there from court
and bring me back for afternoon fines court. Must ask
Mike who else knew about trip.*

Father Peter saw that Bessie had added in red biro, 'Who
were the men at the funeral?'

Father Peter frowned. What did Bessie mean about Sam
being murdered? He had thought Sam had just drowned
at sea, probably because he was drunk and had fallen
overboard. That's what Mike had told him. And why had
Bessie been in touch with the Ministry of Agriculture and
Fisheries? He continued reading.

Monday, 21st May
collect money for bench party.
Friday, 8th June
Jenny's party for the Thursday bench at the Marina.
Friday, 13th July
*Hot, hot day. Sad to see young Joe Hennessy in
Juvenile. Another month and he'll be 17. Asked for
reports in 3 weeks. Give him a fright. Have asked to
stay on the case. Shame about Joe, he was a good kid.
His date of birth is 15th August. Made me very sad.*

Father Peter felt the tears trickling down his face. He had not realised Bessie had been one of the magistrates judging Joe. The boy had been one of his brightest pupils in primary school. The headmaster of the Catholic comprehensive predicted a brilliant future for him. Then Old Nick had moved into the boy's life. He had gone missing that summer of 1990. Father Peter did not know whether he was alive or dead. He checked regularly with the agencies but there was no word about him. He had even managed to get his photograph on the 'Missing' page in the *Big Issue*, but to no avail. Yes, Father Peter thought, he would definitely pray to Saint Jude tonight.

Friday, 20th July
Meet Mark at Chichester Theatre. His birthday treat for me.
Friday, 3rd August
The big 60. Stella picking me up at 4.30.

Father Peter rubbed his eyes. Friday, the third of August, 1990. The memory of that period was branded forever in his mind.

It had been so hot. The hottest summer he could ever remember. A summer when environmentalists warned about a global warming and an increase in the ozone hole. They also prophesied a rise in sea levels. The people in the South of England looked eagerly forward to a future when the olive and vine would flourish in their area and they could enjoy a Mediterranean lifestyle. Hoteliers dreamed of future tourism and applied for the right to commercialise the beaches. They wanted to erect parasols as they did in the South of France or Spain. Their requests were turned down by the local councils. They were told it was crown property and everyone had the right of access.

The hoteliers' dreams faded as they watched itinerants,

the homeless and the unemployed settle like a colony of seals along the edge of the sewerage-slicked shore.

That evening he had walked to the end of the Palace Pier on his arcade patrol, searching for three primary-school boys whose parents had forbidden them to come down to the arcades during the holidays. When they spotted him they had fled. He decided to walk back along the promenade and up West Street to make sure they hadn't tried to hide in the arcades there.

Standing at the end of the pier, he looked back through the shimmering heat haze towards the seafront. Even the boarded-up, bank-repossessed buildings looked prosperous in the rich orange sunlight. He watched large families of Indian day-trippers wandering along the stretch of seafront between the pier and the Marina and marvelled at the bright daubs of coloured saris among the hordes of young people wearing bleached blue jeans. Miniskirts were being worn again, he noticed.

That day he had felt so safe from Old Nick's temptations, banished as he believed for ever after his forty-second year. That hot summer in 1990, having reached the age of sixty-five, he thought any recurrence of the fight was impossible.

It had been like a hand reaching up from the deepest, darkest, unknown chasm to his lofty spiritually smug state. Lust. Had it grown in the sweltering heat, an unnoticed seed fed by the moisture in his aged folds of skin? Whatever the reason, the force of it shocked him.

When he had confessed to it after his first experience at the age of forty-two, the priest hearing his confession had laughed. 'Well thank God you're human, Peter. I was beginning to think you were going to end up a saint.'

He had watched others fighting various sexual predilections during his younger years but had never been bothered himself. At one time he thought God had not meant him to

23

feel arousal, perhaps arranged it so that certain glands were permanently under the control of prayer. The obsessional nature of the beast when he first experienced it in middle age appalled him, and he fought the body by prayer and mental diversion until the madness passed. The power of the late summer lust in 1990 horrified him. It was more devious than before. It had waited until he was watching some innocent brightly dressed tourists. He was listening to the sounds of the soft materials and the swishing of women's skirts as they walked along the pier when Old Nick declared war.

And it took a murder, a horrible, cruel murder, to find out why Old Nick could catch him so late in life.

August the third was the last entry in the diary.

Father Peter closed the Filofax and got up from his chair. His legs felt stiff, his ribs ached and his brain seemed so befuddled that it was unlikely he would be able to work out a simple crossword puzzle, never mind the curious references in Bessie's diary.

He drew back the curtains and looked across the snow-covered rooftops. There were no stars to be seen, just a heavy blackness of hidden snow waiting to cover all human design. It was possible that there had been four murders he thought, remembering Bessie's reference to Sam. As far as he knew, the police had never made an arrest. Were the murders connected, he wondered, or were they just random? And who had sent him the Filofax?

2

During the eleven-hour flight travelling British Airways World Traveller, Stella Potocki felt as if she had developed elephantine legs. The long walk from the outer perimeters of Gatwick's north terminal had at least eased the tightness of the skin round her ankles, and she noticed with amusement how she had developed the splay-footed loping gait of the West Indians. After island-hopping in the Caribbean for five weeks her blood was petrified by the icy blast that greeted passengers leaving the warm air-conditioned airport.

She now regretted the vanity that had determined her choice of white jeans and open-necked sweater, but she felt so good, so unusually glamorous with this wonderful dusky tan, that she wanted to enjoy every moment of it. Even her dark chestnut hair had light sunstreaks. Her favourite pink lipstick had never looked so good. In fact, she thought smugly, for forty-three, I look bloody sexy.

She had finished writing the features on Barbados, Jamaica and St Lucia and faxed them back to London, but stolen a week's holiday before starting the thousand-word article on Grenada. She had spent most of the flight going through her notes on Carricou folklore, and now, while she zipped up her yellow padded bomber jacket, she realised that her gloves and scarf were at the bottom of the holdall.

As she dragged her luggage across the long-stay car park, she decided that if she could sleep for most of the day – it was after all a Sunday – then work flat out Monday and Tuesday she could meet the Wednesday deadline. She would travel up to London, fix a few other meetings for that day, and present it in person to the editor. She had slowed down so much in sympathy with the islands that she had been able to write only after sundown. And then only for an hour before the earth threw back the heat absorbed during the day. She would then make her way to a restaurant to eat some delicious creole dish before returning to her beachfront room and flopping into another heavy sleep.

Stella could see the old Saab's elongated shape and frozen, crooked aerial, standing out among all the other snow-covered vehicles. Solid and reliable, the engine started at the first turn of the ignition.

The grit lorries had been along the M23 but she still took great care on the motorway. She was tired. Her neck ached from straining to see the in-flight film, and the last thing she needed was to go into a skid. Apart from a Post Office van that hurtled past her, most of the early morning traffic was travelling slowly on the inside lane.

She wondered why Post Office van-drivers always drove so recklessly, whatever the weather. The legacy for serving on the bench for five years was her awesome respect for speed limits. Occasionally she liked to take a chance, risk being caught, for the sheer joy of cruising at ninety miles an hour, but after a couple of miles of exhilaration the old warning would sound in her head. Endorsement, penalty points, fine, totting up and disposable income.

When she resigned from the bench, it had been the end of an era, the end of a time when she had felt at one with her soul. She had renounced the need to give service to the community, the need that had encouraged some of the finer traits in her character. After shedding the persona of Justice of the Peace, she had joined the marketplace; then, disillusioned with the limitations of that philosophy, had returned to her own familiar state of rebellion, embracing her natural cynicism towards anything that represented the Establishment.

She was just in time to catch the nine o'clock news on the car radio. Most of the talk was about the weather conditions. There had been gales in December, floods in January and now, in February, she had returned to snow – apparently covering the whole eastern part of Britain. The south-east was particularly bad according to the newscaster. There was a brief extract from a speech given by Prince Charles on architecture reflecting a nation's spiritual life, and a mention of a profitable trade agreement with South Africa.

She switched off and enjoyed watching for the familiar landmarks guiding her on her way home.

Home. Coming home. She always thought of Brighton as home.

Whenever she had arrived back from Africa during all the years she was writing for *The Times*, she had never thought of the flat in London as home. Just as 'our place in London', never home. Now there were free elections in South Africa, no more apartheid. A decade ago, when she was last there, it had been so different. She smiled wryly at the changes in her life during the last ten years. Ten years ago she had arrived back at Gatwick broken by fear. Fear had almost destroyed her. Fear of another beating, more questioning, fear of being rescued from a prison while covered in one's own excreta. She had prayed, whimpering as if she were a child in the middle of a nightmare, but it was anger that saved her. The rage of losing two teeth gave her the determination to survive.

She slid her tongue along the metallic shape covering the roof of her mouth. She was so used to it now that it never bothered her. Except for toffees. They were a luxury to be enjoyed alone, at home.

When she had been arrested, she'd been interviewing

two members of the ANC in Soweto. Misinformation had been given out about her disappearance. According to the authorities, she had been captured by black militants. Filthy and stinking to hell, she had finally been dumped by them, late at night, into the most dangerous area of Soweto. She knew they had hoped she might be killed by some of the youths roaming the area.

Luckily, one of the gang of aggressive teenagers who had found her recognised her from her picture in the newspapers. She had been taken to a shack where she'd been cleaned up, before being smuggled out to the Johannesburg *Sunday Times*. Once she was safely there, the journalists had arranged her flight out. As she was leaving, two steely-eyed officials had told her that she was banned – no visa would be permitted in the future.

After a month's captivity in a South African jail, Stella had believed the old axiom that nothing worse could ever happen to her. It could – and did. Within a week of her return to England, her lover, Colin, had left her for a younger woman, and Tadeusz, her father, who had suffered a heart attack when it was announced she was missing, died. She was in a state of mental breakdown when she returned home, back to Brighton, craving the sanctuary of any kind of permanence in life. She had wandered round her father's rambling, gaudily decorated house, not knowing where to start clearing up. Bessie had come immediately, and mothered her, as she always had, right through Stella's childhood. She offered Stella a loving refuge from turmoil and rejection.

Bessie had helped her dispose of all the exotic birds her father kept in his large aviary, and the tropical plants from his homemade shambles of a greenhouse. Together they sorted out the selection of garish plates and mismatching furniture bartered from different antique-dealers in Brighton – 'Always deal in cash, darlink' – and hidden whenever the VAT people arrived.

Stella kept a few things. His new Saab, his telescope, which he kept for watching the movements of the moon. She had climbed into the spider-run attic and found his most precious Polish possessions, souvenirs of his battle in Monte Cassino, all hidden among old socks stuffed with cash skimmed from the restaurant's takings.

Bessie had helped her to sell the house and restaurant, and find a simple apartment which Stella furnished in the plainest style she could. She had taken comfort in listening to the older woman's philosophies, just as she had as a child, when Bessie would tell her fairy stories, creating the homeliness she craved and never received from her own mother. Halina had always been too busy slavishly following her husband's ambitions to attend to her daughter's needs.

During Stella's early childhood every motherly gesture from Halina had seemed like an effort to be made. Stella had felt she was an unwelcome diversion from Halina's true need in life, which was the approval of her husband. It had been easy to transfer all her childish affections to Bessie. Bessie, the great mother figure, making sure she had her tea, collecting her for brownies, helping her with her homework, advising her about boys, always there. It was Bessie and her brothers and sisters who accompanied Tadeusz to the valedictory service when she collected her first-class honours degree.

Halina had died when Stella was fifteen. She was worn out from working six days a week with Tadeusz, while trying to run a home. After an intracerebral haemorrhage, she spent six months lost in a Polish world of half-dreams, her mind flitting between reality and madness. She was obsessed about emptying, checking and replacing the odd contents of her handbag, or hiding food. Stale pieces of bread wrapped in toilet paper were always to be found at the back of her hospital locker. And the cruellest experience for Stella was that Halina, during her last few months, treated her as a stranger.

Aware of the dangers to her own mind after all the stress following the African experience, Stella had taken refuge in respectability. Through Bessie, she'd clung to the welcoming arms of old values, duty, honour and service, to the acts of faith, hope and charity. She sought peace of mind through the ordinary.

Her old schoolfriends, Maureen and Jenny, had also helped her to pick up the tattered pieces of her life. They had introduced her to a new social routine, and a gentler way of living. They cast a spell, an illusion, of back-to-basics, which was what she desperately needed.

She had gone back to Saint Mary Magdalene's and Father Peter, the once handsome, blond priest with penetrating blue eyes, whom she, Maureen and Jenny had adored as children, and fancied wildly as teenagers. Once back to the mass with the comforting smell of incense, her wounded psyche was restored to a new self. Gone was the daredevil, the thirty-three-year old liberated woman in a man's world. Gone was the sophisticated traveller, the heroine of her own romantic story enjoying meetings with Colin in hotels in different countries, en route to another war or another political scandal in Africa. No more mad weeks in London where they would savour each other's exploits, read each other's copy, make love and, as the well-known talented couple, dance to the music of fame.

She found she had lost her nerve. The memory of the month in the South African jail had become like some cruel aversion therapy, with the effect of instant apprehension every time she tried to write. The extended sick leave from *The Times* became a permanent redundancy.

It was Bessie who'd proposed that she become a magistrate. 'It'll be good for you Stella. It'll focus your mind,' she said. 'And we need streetwise career women, not just bored middle-class wives. We need people who know poverty and understand what it can do to people, women who aren't impressed by modulated vowels and hyphenated names.'

Urged on by Maureen and Jenny – a rich bored wife, a fact conveniently forgotten by Bessie – who were already JPs on the same bench, Stella eventually agreed to be put forward for selection. So, in 1986, the year after she'd arrived back in Brighton, she found herself, having completed the training, standing in front of a judge and swearing the Oath of Allegiance, followed by the Judicial Oath.

'I swear by Almighty God that I will well and truly serve our Sovereign Lady Queen Elizabeth the Second, in the office of Justice of the Peace, and I will do right to all manner of people after the laws and usages of the realm without fear or favour, affection or ill will.'

She could see Father Peter, Bessie, Maureen and Jenny, seated together in the courtroom and smiling up at her. As she took her place beside the judge and listened to his speech about the importance of magistrates and justice, she thought of her mother. She would have been so proud.

Stella had loved and despised her mother. Always resented the need to be nursed better in illness, hated the sense of occasion her mother felt at her first menstruation, as if by the sign of blood Stella would become more like her. She watched her mother cringe and whimper round the restaurant, referring to her father as 'Mai oosband, the chef,' until Stella had wanted to puke. Once, after watching her grovelling round what she called 'a reel Eenglish lady' – some matronly snob from the outer suburbs of Brighton – she had shouted at her. Her mother had raged back, which took Stella by suprise. Halina was never known to fight back.

'Have you ever counted my tips Shtella? You get tips because everyone wants to look down on someone. What do I care if they look down on me?'

'I care,' Stella screamed at her,

'Well, let's hope you never have to plead for food, as I have done. Let's hope you never have to be frightened for your life, as I have been. Let's hope you never know what it's like to be a refugee, a stranger in a country, dependent on the people feeling sorry for you. Perhaps if you knew, you would not be so much Miss High and Mighty.'

Stella had remembered her words when her tongue was swollen with thirst and she was pleading with her jailors for some water. Her self-imposed penance for her past callousness towards her mother was to light a candle after the Polish twelve o'clock mass every Sunday at Saint Mary Magdalene's.

Her father, she knew, would have been horrified at her becoming a magistrate. Tadeusz had rowed with Bessie when she became one. 'What you bloody doing Bessie? What you want with these bloody busybodies. They come into the restaurant, looking in the toilets, inspecting my kitchen, to see if I, a hard-working restaurant-owner, should have a licence. What you want with these people?'

He used to drive like the Post Office van-driver, Stella thought. She had once gone with him to the London market, late at night, after the restaurant had closed, to pick up boxes of chickens. On the return journey, his driving had been terrible. She heard some bumping sounds and realised that the chickens had been falling off the car. They had to stop and go back for a mile or so collecting the gleaming white carcasses from the road.

Her thoughts returned to the present as the familiar Sussex downs came into view. Another half an hour and she would be in her eighth-floor apartment overlooking the Marina. She remembered that the supermarket in the Marina was open on a Sunday. She would be able to get some fresh bread, a carton of milk and a few eggs for later.

Home, back home.

She could already taste the sweetness of an English cup of tea.

The red light on her answering-machine was blinking. The tinny electronic woman's voice told her, 'You have seven messages.' The first was from the features editor of the *Mail*, wanting to know if she was free to go on a day trip to Prague with Air Tours. The second was from the editor of the *Saturday Times* Travel Supplement who wanted her to cut her Grenada feature by two hundred and fifty words to accommodate more advertising. Stella cursed. It was always the same. Over the last few years she had built up a good reputation as a freelance travel writer, with the result that the holiday firms bought in when they knew she was writing the piece.

The third message was from her dentist reminding her of her appointment on the following Thursday. The fourth, a wrong number. A hospital staff nurse telling some husband that his wife was coming out of hospital at one o'clock, so could he pick her up. Stella sipped her tea, wondering what happened, how long the wife had waited and whether the poor ignorant husband was believed when summoned again. No one ever admits to making a mistake in the National Health Service these days, she thought.

Stella hated hospitals. She still remembered 1967, and the last month of her mother's life. She would visit the hospital every day after school, with a clean nightie, or fruit in a carrier bag. She would try to be cheerful when greeted by malevolent eyes, a puckering chicken's arse of a mouth and Halina's spitting rages as she fought her brain's creeping death. Sometimes, Halina would treat Stella like one of her 'reel Eenglish ladies', sinking into her pillow subserviently and smiling stupidly as she asked Stella what she wanted 'for starters'.

Stella had felt nothing at the funeral. She was caught up

in her father's grief so could mercifully be seen to be crying, but, apart from missing the sound of her querulous voice, the only effect her mother's death had on her was to make Stella determined never to be like her in any way whatsoever.

The fifth message was from a BBC reporter, Mike Harwood. He was an old friend of Colin's, and was just back from covering the troubles in Sarajevo. He had been visiting Brighton to see his father, a fortnight ago, and wanted to know if he could take her for lunch, or, if she could not make lunch, would she like to come to a party? Thank goodness he'd left his telephone number, Stella thought. She wrote it down quickly in her telephone and address book. Two years ago he had sent her a change-of-address card which she'd immediately lost. She was glad he had telephoned. It would be stimulating to talk to a war correspondent again.

During the last few days of her holiday in Grenada, union troubles had broken out among the hotel staff. Apparently the service charges weren't reaching those who had trudged across the sands with fruit punch, carried the triple-decker toasted sandwiches to lounging tourists or brought the Coca Cola with a smile. Stella had yearned to get involved. She found herself asking questions about the impending elections and gathering information about the political feeling on the street. The excitement caught her by surprise and she wondered whether she was ready, at last, to go back to political journalism. Or should she concentrate on spices, sunsets, clear seas, reefs teeming with bright-coloured fish, and ignore the small valiant island paper, *The Voice*, trying to raise funds against libel.

At the time, she decided that the feature was about rainforests, fruit, calypso music, steel bands and nutmeg. And all things that are nice. That was what a well-mannered travel writer was made of. Especially if she wanted another highly paid job. These days, she thought ruefully, everyone seemed to be in the have-a-nice-day, don't-rock-the-boat, don't-bite-the-hand-that-feeds-you mood, and she had to survive. But her instincts and her scent for political change had definitely returned, reawakening the old familiar restlessness.

She wanted to write that, like the rainclouds reaching for the forest, the whispers and drumbeats of antagonism would return. She could feel it, the resentment, she could see the peeling decaying St George's. The real story she had found on her trip to Grenada was the message she read in the beach vendors' eyes. It said, 'When do I get some of the affluent action?'

The sixth voice was that of the editor of a women's magazine wanting her to call her as soon as possible. She had left the message four days ago. Stella made a note to call her first thing Monday morning. The magazine paid really well for a feature and she didn't want to miss it.

The seventh was a call from Father Peter, wanting her to contact him urgently. There was a pause, some laboured breathing before he said, 'I don't know what to do, Stella. I've got Bessie's Filofax.'

Burning heat from the mug of tea brought her back out of her stunned state. She replayed the message. Father Peter sounded as she felt, breathless and shocked.

She had pushed 1990 out of her mind, trying only to remember the good times with Bessie. Now the sense of loss overwhelmed her. She paced backwards and forwards in front of the balcony windows, looking towards the Marina with its snow-covered boats, searching for a distraction from wave upon wave of anger, horror, guilt and regret.

If she had not tried so hard to please her, Bessie might still be alive.

Stella rested her forehead against the cold glass balcony doors, trying to push away the horrors of 1990, and attempting to conjure up the more pleasant memories again.

The four years spent serving on the bench with Bessie

had been a time of renewal. Stella had learned a great deal of respect for many people with whom she would not otherwise have come into contact. She found being a magistrate a challenge to her powers of concentration. As a journalist she knew how to sift out facts, casually interrogate, and by fair means or foul get the answers she needed to write her story. But to find herself restricted by court procedure, so that she was unable to find out anything that was not part of the correct ritual of what was or what was not presented as facts relevant to the case, was at first infuriating. 'It's like playing a bloody fruit machine, Bessie,' she complained, when she first started sitting and was fooled by the great performances of seasoned villains time and time again. She became used to the often comic dramas in court. The grimacing of prisoners in the dock, the shaking of the head, like seasoned politicians knowing the camera is on them when another person is putting forward their case. She watched policemen roll their eyes to the heavens as they listened to a witness for the defence perjuring themselves without shame.

'Why aren't people charged with perjury?' she demanded, as one person after another flagrantly lied in court. 'Why bother with the oath if lying is an accepted means of prosecution or defence?'

Bessie was popular with most of the magistrates and was tipped to be the next chairman of the bench. She was up against Charles Nightingale, a Tory supporter, the youngest son of a very old fishing family. His brother had originally run a fleet of fishing boats from Hastings until he was killed in a car accident. Charles then took over the company. Up until then he had made his living first by dealing in slot machines, then by becoming involved with hotels and leisure complexes. He had become friendly with many highly placed government ministers and was often seen with them at high society functions. He was also very involved with the Freemasons. Stella wanted Bessie to win the vote, so did Maureen, but Jenny favoured Charles Nightingale. Stella was suprised, especially when Jenny began making fun of Bessie.

'Oh come on Stella, Bessie's too po for words. And you can't have a fat chairman of the bench. I mean she really ought to go on a diet or do something about herself. She farted in the traffic court the other day. I mean, I ask you. The poor policeman giving evidence in the witness box nearly died. He turned bright red, and stared at his notebook, trying not to laugh. She was coughing and then we heard it. Loud, like a motor bike. It bounced round the walls. And do you know? – she just smiled at the court. The crown prosecutor kept looking so hard at her notes that she nearly went boss-eyed. The toerag up for no insurance had his mouth open. And Charlie Nightingale generously said, 'Pardon.' I think that was really nice of him, don't you?'

Maureen had been helpless with laughter, but later said to Stella, 'Jenny could always tell a funny story. But I wouldn't like to leave the room when she's in a witty mood.'

A gust of wind brought fresh snow on to the balcony. Thick flakes fell steadily, blanketing Stella's view of the Marina. If only she hadn't tried so hard to please Bessie, but Bessie gave her so much of her time, introduced her to so much richness in life. Stella helped Bessie with her favourite charity, the soup runs on the beach for the homeless and the events organised for Saint Mary Magdalene's, with Maureen and Jenny.

Bessie had also been right about Stella benefiting from serving as a magistrate. The sheer challenge of coping with the sadness, the humour and holding on to the facts through red herrings and other distractions, eventually pulled her poor, bruised mental faculties into a focused, probing, self-disciplined whole again. After her first eighteen months, the terrors from the experiences in the African jail began to recede and she started writing the occasional piece again for *Dziennik Polski*, the Polish daily and weekly newspapers, based in Hove.

Dziennik Polski was first printed in Scotland in 1940 and moved offices to Hove in 1957.

When Stella had just left university in 1973, and was employed as a researcher on the *Sunday Times*, she was lucky to get the occasional 'extra reporting by,' or 'extra research by' in small print at the bottom of a feature. She had often helped the staff at *Dziennik Polski* then, during her holidays, and that summer of 1973, the Polish newspaper gave her a by-line. She had written a feature dealing with troubles between Iceland and Britain over fishing, and a young MP called John Prescott, who was desperately trying to prevent any fisherman being killed. Stella had been so excited about having her first real by-line that she had wanted to show it to Bessie, but that was the summer Bessie was away for a few months on some trade union course. By the time Bessie had returned to Brighton, Stella had been sent on her first overseas assignment, in Mozambique.

It had been an extension of the discipline in court, writing for *Dziennik Polski* again. Because she had to think in another language – not difficult for her – ninety percent of all second-generation Poles were bilingual; it removed the fear of writing. Her confidence began to return and she had offered to help Bessie write her reports for the Magistrates' Association.

She wondered what was in Bessie's Filofax. Had Father Peter found any clues that could identify her murderer?

The Filofax had been stolen on Bessie's sixtieth birthday, the third of August, 1990.

Stella had wanted to give Bessie something really special so she had bought two tickets for Glyndebourne.

The third of August turned out to be the hottest day of the year. Ninety-nine degrees Fahrenheit. Hotter than the weather records of 1911 and 1976. The third of August. The day after Iraq 'rescued' Kuwait, giving Iraq the control of twenty-five percent of the world's oil. Stella had dressed for the opera wondering all the time who among the journalists she knew would be sent to cover the inevitable war. She had stood on her balcony gasping for a breath of cool air and trying to mould the look of enthusiasm on to her face for Bessie's sake. To be watching Strauss's *Capriccio*, listening to the argument about whether poetry or music is more important, when every newsroom on every newspaper would be looking up cuttings on the Middle East, seemed extraordinary. She had booked a place in the Nether Wallop restaurant for the interval and ordered Bessie's favourite starter, Parma ham and melon, which she knew would be followed by cold salmon, new potatoes and salad, then strawberries and cream. Cold Chablis in an iced bucket and everything would be perfect for her.

At four thirty in the afternoon, she collected Bessie. The Saab was all polished and gleaming for the occasion, but, even with the roof open, the heat was unbearable.

Bessie was waiting by her front gate, her chubby face glowing with excitement. Her grey hair was styled, her plump body well corsetted, so that her black sequined chiffon evening dress hung beautifully.

'Thirty-five pounds in Hannington's sale, Stella, what do you think?'

She tottered towards the car in new evening sandals, showing off her recently manicured nails.

'So what do you think?'

'You look really elegant.'

'Got to, haven't I?' she laughed, delighted with herself.'
Got to fit in with all the nobs. God it's hot.'

The world-famous, small opera theatre, part of a fifteenth-century private house, is situated on the Sussex downs. As they parked the Saab between two chauffeur-driven cars, a Rolls-Royce and a Bentley, Bessie beamed at Stella.

'Well, for two slum kids, we haven't done too badly, have we?'

From clumps of trees, rooks called, sheep grazed on a nearby hillside, the air was heavy with expensive perfume as they wandered round beautiful gardens and lily ponds before making for the Long Bar for some Pimms.

'Oh Stella, it's Arcadia,' Bessie whispered.

She delighted in seeing well-known people dressed in their finery. There were a lot of Tory MPs, guests of various corporations' hospitality.

'Villains are everywhere these days,' Bessie joked.

She was an old-fashioned socialist, Stella mused at the time. She believed in the monarchy, accepted completely a hierarchical system, never resented people like Jenny who were rich, but believed passionately that the working classes should have their just rewards. Her dedication to trade unionism came first before any party politics. As area manager of the local branch of TSSA (Transport Salaried Staff Association) representing the Southern region of British Rail, she had fought hard for the staff. To walk along a platform at Brighton station with her was like walking beside the Queen. There was always a chorus of 'All right Bessie?', 'How are ye, gal?' 'Good to see ye.' She was also respected by all the court clerks and was known to fight for their interests when serving on the courts committee.

As usual, the Glyndebourne theatre was packed to capacity. Even with the doors left wide open, the audience was stifled by the heat. Fans of every size and shape fluttered like moths in the dark. The opera was being sung in the original German but had English supertitles.

'Thank God for that,' said Bessie.

They were sitting in the centre of Row P in the stalls. When the cigar was lit in the first act while Flamand, the

40

composer, Olivier, the poet, and La Roche, the producer, discuss who is the most important in entertainment, Stella became overwhelmed by claustrophobia and feelings of panic. She felt perspiration trickling down the back of her green silk trouser-suit. Her scalp prickled with what seemed like underground springs welling to life and pouring down her neck. Bessie's laughter stopped the panic. La Roche was pretending to be merely concerned with 'giving the public what it wants'.

'That'll go down well with the Tories,' she whispered.

During the long interval they were lucky enough to have been given a table placed right under one of the fans that were stategically placed across the ceiling. After coffee, they heard the five minute bell for the start of Act Two.

'Stella,' Bessie said, her forehead covered in perspiration. 'Stella, I really appreciate this wonderful treat. But, truthfully, we are here to enjoy ourselves, aren't we?

'Yes.'

'Well, my support hose are strangling my knees, my corset is as wet as a dishcloth, and I think if I go back in there I'll die.'

Stella began to giggle. 'Do you want to go?'

'Would you mind dreadfully?'

'I can't think of anything more wonderful.'

'Oh Stella, I've got some homemade lemonade in the fridge. We could sit in the back garden. I could get out of my corset.'

They had run across the grounds, passing people returning with their picnic baskets. Bessie, with her skirts lifted, was laughing uncontrollably. The chauffeurs seeing them running towards the car looked most alarmed, which started Bessie off again.

They drove away, windows open, rebelliously leaving the seatbelts undone. They sped along winding country lanes, watching the largest, deepest-orange, harvest moon rise, as the red sun sank into the west, casting shadows over rich-harvested fields.

Stella stood by the balcony windows weeping at the memory of that mad journey home. She had never been so happy, never laughed so much with Bessie as she had that evening. By some incredibly agile wriggling, Bessie managed to pull off the offending tights so that when they arrived at her home she was carrying the limp hose in one hand and her evening bag in the other.

Then they saw that her front door was open.

'Don't touch anything,' Stella warned her.

While Bessie went into the kitchen, Stella rang the police.

'An amateur,' Bessie said. 'He's had some cold beer, left the can on the table to let me know he's been, and eaten a banana. I can't think what he's taken.'

The police arrived within five minutes. Also, a young reporter from the local paper turned up. Stella did not notice him. She was with Bessie checking for anything that might have been stolen.

Bessie's purse was still on the bed where she'd left it, the money untouched.

'I know this is where I put some coins in my evening purse,' Bessie said to a policewoman. 'Then I went down-stairs to the front room. Oh hell . . .' She rushed downstairs. Stella and the policewoman followed. The other police were at the back of the house, inspecting the small window the burglar had forced open in order to reach the main kitchen window's latch. 'My Filofax,' Bessie shouted, 'and my credit cards. Oh, no, the Magistrates' Year Book. Oh my God.'

'Is the Magistrates' Year Book important, Miss Baker?' The young reporter asked her. Before Stella could stop her, the overwrought Bessie replied, 'Of course it's important. It has the names and addresses of all the magistrates and clerks. You don't want that information falling into the hands of the wrong people.'

Next day, while the national newspapers discussed the problems of Kuwait, on the front page of the Saturday local paper, the headlines were, FEAR STALKS THE JUST OF BRIGHTON.

The article mentioned that the police had recovered the credit cards from a known dealer. It also made a lot of the fact that the Magistrates' Year Book was still missing. Bessie was quoted as saying, 'You don't want that information falling into the hands of the wrong people.'

Then the phone calls began.

Stella felt as if salted peanuts were rolling around under her eyelids. Pain darted across her skull. It was now eleven-thirty on Sunday morning – she had been travelling since four o'clock on Saturday afternoon and had not slept on the plane. The combination of shock from Father Peter's message and travel fatigue was too much for her. She did not want to remember any more. She wanted to forget all the 'if onlys' and 'what ifs' that she had plagued herself with in the past. Wearily she headed for the bedroom, for sleep and oblivion.

It was too hot and the lurking images were trying to come through to the surface of her dream. Stella's mind scrambled into an escape route of pleasant recollections. Was she still in Grenada, stealing the extra holiday instead of returning home straight away to finish the feature? No, her brain reasoned, she was in Brighton, and she had turned the central heating thermostat up too much. The memory of Thursday, the sixteenth of August, 1990, was pushing forward. Perspiration streamed from her scalp into her eyes. She had to wake up, had to stop the vivid pictures emerging from the darkness.

She stumbled out of bed and padded through the hallway to the temperature control. It had to be suppressed. She had to keep the squirming, wriggling nightmare under the heap of all the other horrors locked deep in the vaults of her subconscious. To let just one escape would be to unleash on herself her own damnation.

The kettle took an age to boil. She switched on Radio Three and listened to the beginning of Mahler's Symphony Number Five while she clattered about the kitchen collecting teabags, sugar and milk. She kept a carton of duty-free Rothmans in the hall cupboard. They were there for an emergency – she had given up smoking two years ago. It *was* an emergency, she decided. She heard the kettle boil as she was trying to rip the cellophane off the packet.

It was four in the afternoon, and while she had slept the snow had covered the grit laid earlier on the coast road.

Stella took a deep drag at the filter-tip. The hot tea and nicotine scorched her throat. She tried counting the frozen masts in the Marina, but the memories seeped into her brain. Flashing images darting in and out of her mind.

Four in the morning had been the time of the first of the telephone calls. They had begun on the Sunday night after the burglary. She had picked up the telephone, said 'Hello, yes?' and then the line had gone dead. Just as she began to drift back to sleep the ringing started again. The calls came during the day and night. She remembered the jangling nerves, the rage at this unseen caller who would wait just the right amount of time before replacing the receiver. Wait until the imagination was fired, the scream about to be uttered, 'Who the hell are you, you creep?'

The calls came at midnight to unsettle her before sleep, then in the early hours to pull her out of the drifting floating relief that she became used to instead of sleep. She would wake into a sour-tasting panic.

Bessie was getting them as well. After a week, they both decided to report the calls to the police. The nuisance-calls operator rang and told them the drill. She told them that, whenever they answered the telephone and suspected that it might be a nuisance call, they were immediately to dial one. She said as soon as they did this, it would alert the telephone system to begin tracing the call. They were also told that any emergency call made from their telephones would be listed for a direct link-up with the police. Because of the robbery a superintendent was put in charge.

Stella became so nervous every time a call came through to her that she often reacted clumsily and she spent most of the day apologising to either the telephone operator or friends for jamming the line.

They found out that several magistrates were getting the nuisance calls, including Maureen and Jenny. Bessie had become quite cross with Jenny, who was making a huge drama out of it. Bessie advised everyone to report any calls to the police and to the nuisance-calls operator as she had done. Then, just when Stella had been about to change her telephone number, quite suddenly they stopped. They stopped on Thursday, the sixteenth of August. The day Bessie was murdered.

She didn't want to remember any more. She had smoked six cigarettes and her chest hurt.

The straining sound of a car's engine revving, followed by the screaming of wheels, drew her attention along the seafront to where a small Ford had become stuck in a drift. She watched the passengers get out and attempt to rock the vehicle back into the middle of the road. She was grateful for the unknown travellers' exertions, grateful for their very existence. It had distracted her from the dreaded memory.

The sky was darkening, streetlights became smeared orange halos against a skyline of pewter-grey sea.

A baby cried in one of the flats. Stella watched a light go on and turned the telescope in the direction of a new diversion.

A young mother was picking up the yelling infant. She

walked to the window and looked across the sea. She looked so peaceful with the child nestling into her neck. An instinctive awareness of being watched made her turn her head in Stella's direction, forcing Stella to dart back from the window and the telescope. She hadn't been seen, hadn't been caught watching someone else's life.

She was a voyeur, a reporter of other people's lives, other people's holidays, intrigues and corruptions. A detached eye, seeing, observing and telling. Her own life, thoughts and actions she enclosed more and more to herself. Her smile was now a barrier between her and the world. She could recount a story, behave well at a party, and no one could see the seething rage about society, the anger she felt about politics. No one suspected that she entered into such great dark depressions that could occasionally twist every moment of joy from her life.

From the kitchen, she could hear the strains of the third section of the symphony, the adagietto, one of Bessie's favourite pieces of music. She wondered whether she should make some scrambled eggs, anything to avoid reliving that Thursday. The images were creeping back. She lit another cigarette, trying to deflect the memory by pretending that she was back in Grenada sitting on the veranda of her beachfront room, listening to the gentle movements of the sea. It was no good. Her mind was becoming filled with the memory of that terrible morning.

She had woken refreshed by a south-easterly breeze wafting through the veranda doors. She had left them wide open the previous night. It had been so humid that she had half expected a storm. She had slept naked in the position of a starfish trying to let every part of her skin breathe.

After a shower and breakfast, she had picked out a cool linen navy summer suit for court. Depending on which room one was in, one could be blasted by cold air or roasted to almost suffocation by a totally inadequate air-conditioning

46

system. In some courts the chairmen had to warn the defendants to speak up loudly to be heard above its noise, and in other courtrooms magistrates had been known to fall asleep through the effects of its hum.

That Thursday morning Stella had wanted to get to court early so she could tell Bessie the news about the first travel feature. A week in Rome. She had checked the day before with the editor of the British Airways magazine and he had agreed that she could take a friend. She had known the editor when he worked in Fleet Street. A few weeks previously she had run into him while shopping in the Marina. They'd had a drink and talked of old times, and she had confessed to having lost her nerve. He had then suggested that perhaps she should try to write a simple travel feature. She felt exhilarated and terrified at the same time when he said he would see what he could arrange.

As Stella had set off for the courts she had been thinking about how Bessie would be thrilled. She had been nagging Stella for months about 'getting off your backside and going back to work'.

'I know you're ready to start writing again, Stella,' she said. 'I saw some of your jottings on the back of your court list. Interesting thoughts. I kept them.'

'How did you get my court list?'

'You forgot to tear it up and you left it on the windowsill. So I took it.'

Stella reached the magistrates' carpark by nine-fifteen that morning. Bessie was always in early, at the latest by nine thirty. She was in the middle of chairing a five-day not guilty case. It involved hearing ten witnesses giving evidence about a horrendous assault. This was the fourth day of the hearing and Bessie liked to arrive early, relax with a coffee, talking to the other magistrates and clerks, checking through her notes, and preparing her mind for the case, so she was ready to go into court promptly

47

at ten. And God help any solicitor who was not on time.

She wasn't there.

By nine-forty-five, the court clerk due in Bessie's court was getting anxious. So was Stella. She tried phoning Bessie's home. The number was out of order. As Stella was due in a traffic court and it was easy to replace her, she volunteered to drive to Bessie's home to see if she was all right.

When she reached the house she found the curtains drawn, the milk bottles still on the doorstep and the newspaper stuck in the letterbox. She had laughed out aloud. Bessie had overslept, she thought. Oh boy, was she going to get a fright. She rang the doorbell.

After a few minutes when there was no response she became frightened. She went to the house next door and called the court clerk, who informed the police.

Stella had waited, alternately ringing the doorbell shouting, 'Bessie, Bessie, are you all right?' and biting her nails. She became aware of the heady perfume from the wallflowers in Bessie's front garden and the numbers of bees droning round the flowers. The everyday sounds in the street seemed strange and unreal.

When the police broke in through the door, the first thing Stella noticed was the smell coming from the kitchen and the sound of flies.

One of the policemen tried to stop her going in but she thought she could see a large fish with its mouth open lying across the kitchen floor.

There was blood everywhere, all over the new white tiles and the freshly decorated walls. She could hear herself whimpering, 'Oh my God, oh my God.' And then she realised that what she thought was a fish on the floor was in fact a pale-faced Bessie, dressed in her grey-patterned cotton dressing-gown, with her throat cut.

The gash in the neck had missed the carotid arteries but

severed the jugular veins, so that before Bessie had died she had made an attempt to reach the telephone. Her handmark was smeared against the wall. Even if she had managed to reach the phone it would have been useless – the wire had been ripped from the socket.

During her last dying moments Bessie had drawn an open-ended loop with a dot on the white tiled floor – the primitive sign of the fish – a secret sign of Christians. She had drawn it with her own blood.

And then Stella was screaming. The police were pulling her away. The scenes-of-crime people were arriving, and she was still screaming. Her mouth felt as forced back as that open wound in Bessie's neck. She could feel her own throat gashed into a never-ending howl. And then blackness.

She had woken to the brightness of hospital white lights. Two concerned-looking detectives were sitting in the room. She knew them from magistrates' lectures at police head-quarters in Lewes.

Outside the hospital window white clouds, fluffy and soft as pillows, drifted lazily out to sea. She had been unable to tell them anything that would be of help. Her aching mind only wanted sleep but she felt she had to keep awake. She had realised that the view from the hospital window was the same as the one she'd always seen when her mother was dying.

Stella stubbed out the cigarette she was smoking. Out, the memory was out, exorcised until the next time. She did not feel like eating scrambled eggs now, but she thought she might be able to sleep.

She looked out of the window. The Ford was out of the drift and was inching along the coast road. Exhausted, Stella made her way to the bedroom.

3

The launderette was about two hundred and fifty yards uphill from the church. Father Peter knew Mike would be there early on Monday morning. His communion class was not until after lunch so he had plenty of time to get back, change, and still make some notes. He had wrapped up warmly, wearing two extra pairs of socks inside his wellington boots. The pavement was slippery. That, combined with the weight of his boots, made the walk tiring and hazardous. He was out of breath when he reached the top of the hill.

While he fought to regain power over his lungs, he thought about the Filofax. According to Bessie's diary, she, Mike and Sam were trying to achieve something. But what? And why would Bessie think that anyone would want to murder Sam?

He looked through the steamed-up window of the launderette and saw Mike sitting watching a selection of clothes smear around the glass front of the washing-machine.

What excuse could he use for going into the place? Father Peter wondered.

The old seaman was pleased to see him. 'Hello Father, what brings you here?'

Father Peter rationalised with his conscience. 'I was just passing, on my way to visit someone, when I saw the back of your head. It's cold out.'

51

'Sure is. Sit down for a while, Father, and warm up. My pipes were frozen this morning.'

The old priest heard his knees crack as he perched on a rather uncomfortable plastic chair. 'I'm sorry to hear that.' He caught his breath. 'Are they all right now?'

He was wondering how to broach the subject of Sam when Mike said, 'I was just sitting here thinking of old Sam.'

If ever he had doubted that the Boss was in charge of this operation, Father Peter now repented for his lack of faith. He felt a surge of excitement and fresh confidence. Stammering slightly with the need to pick up his heavenly inspired cue quickly, he said, 'Your friend who drowned?'

'Yes.' Mike sighed. 'Sometimes I miss him. You know, he never could kick the booze.'

'Didn't it land him in court?'

Mike laughed. 'More than once.'

Father Peter tried to sound casual as he said, 'I seem to remember Bessie was worried about him the last time he came up before her.'

'Yeh, well that was a bit of a green rub.'

'Why?'

'Well, he'd been picked up as drunk and disorderly the night before. And he came up before Miss Baker and Charles Nightingale. And he swore at Nightingale, called him – excuse me swearing, Father – he called him an effing hypocrite. Nightingale was going to do him for contempt of court but I believe Miss Baker talked him out of it.'

'How do you know she did that?'

'She told us when we went round to see her.'

'You and Sam went round?'

'Yeh, I was with him in court, you see. I paid his fine for him. He was angry with Nightingale. And I told him to come and tell Miss Baker what he knew. You see, Miss Baker had often talked to me about environmental things, and we thought perhaps she could do something with all her contacts, being a magistrate and that.'

'To do with what?'

'Well, Sam told me that Nightingale was breaking the fishing quotas, and getting the local lads to pick up from his trawlers and drop the catches along the coast. Then vans would take the fish to different buyers. It was bent. Sam didn't mind doing it 'cause he got paid for not fishing. Fifty quid a time. He just saw red when he saw what he thought was a crook judging him.'

'Did Charles Nightingale himself actually pay Sam?'

'No, course not. That would be real carroty. Not even his skippers did that. The money was paid by the chaps in the vans. In that way anyone would think they were buying local-caught fish, you see.'

'Perhaps Nightingale didn't know what was going on.'

'That's exactly what Miss Baker said. She thought Sam was, you know, unreliable. She told Sam there was no reason for Nightingale to break the law.'

'She was right.'

'She said he was already rich with lots of business interests. He didn't need to break the fishing quota. Sam got really bitter and twisted when she said that. He said he didn't expect to be believed, and it was a waste of time coming to someone who sat on the bench with the élite. 'I thought you was one of us,' he said to her. Anyway, she said she'd think about it and get in touch with him through me.'

The washing-machine came to the end of its cycle and commenced a shuddering spin which slowly gathered speed until it was making a continuous, high-pitched noise. Father Peter found it truly awful.

'And did she?' he shouted.

'What?'

'Get in touch with Sam?'

'Yes she did. It was a while after. Around Easter, I think.

She asked me to get him to come and see her.' Father Peter watched Mike unload the machine and divide the clothes. Some were prepared for the drier, the others neatly folded for ironing. He suddenly felt very humble and grateful for his own privileged lifestyle. Mrs Huggins always saw to his washing. There were two things he really hated doing. One was washing up and the other was ironing. Often his heart sank when some good soul who had given him lunch took him up on his offer to help with the washing up. He would force himself to plunge his hands into greasy water and rub a pan with wire wool, his teeth on edge with every movement.

'Yes, it *was* then,' Mike added, 'because I'd just finished redecorating her kitchen. I went down to the beach to tell Sam. And he was going on about the sky being green again.'

'Was he drunk?'

'No, seriously, Father, green. He wasn't drunk, and I've seen it, too, although it was Sam first pointed it out to me. There's a strange green light comes in the sky before a wind blows up. We first saw it that October in 1987, about four in the afternoon before the hurricane hit that night. You remember, it took down Professor Evans's chimney and her roof. I remember Sam saying to me, 'Is it the booze, Mike, or has the sky started to turn green?' I would like to have scared him and said, 'Yes, it's because of the booze – you'd better give it up.' But he was right. His eyes were always good. He could see a moving ship anywhere on the skyline. Haven't you noticed it Father?'

'Can't say I have.'

'The starlings behave differently too. When the green light comes before a gale, those starlings start to make weird patterns in the sky. They go out to sea and wheel into all kinds of figures-of-eight and things. Without sounding blasphemous Father, it's almost like God's warning us about the gales.'

54

Mike sat down and waited while the tumble-drier threw his pants and vests around. Father Peter tried to put the fascinating story of the green light aside and concentrate on gathering more facts. 'Did you go with him to see Bessie?'

'No, I couldn't the night he was going to see her, I was chairing an AA meeting.'

'Did he tell you what happened when he met her?'

Mike sighed. 'Let me see now. It's so long ago. Yes, that's right. I ran into him at the supermarket. He was buying some cans of beer. Must have been a couple of weeks later. He said Miss Baker had arranged for someone to go with him to get evidence.'

'Who?'

'He didn't know. He was going to meet them near the groyne where he kept his boat. Someone Miss Baker said she could trust. I asked him if it was the police. He said he didn't know.'

'Was that the last time you saw him before he died?'

'No, I saw him once more. I went down to his hut – you know, the one he'd dug into the shingle.'

Father Peter smiled. He remembered Sam thwarting the 1960s by-laws by digging deep into the shingle and inserting a small hut. All one could see when walking along the beach was what appeared to be a lock-up for tackle, standing two feet high from the ground. But the side opened to reveal a stepladder going down about five feet. And down at the bottom of the ladder old Sam would be sitting, brewing tea on his primus stove. Numbers of old Truefood tins were lined around his hut. They contained tea, coffee, biscuits and sugar. Often he had sat on Sam's dinghy, drinking scalding orange tea from a tin mug and eating digestive biscuits. The old man's face and arms were weatherbeaten but what always amused Father Peter was the glimpse of white neck when he turned his head.

'Don't believe in all this sunbathing,' he would say. 'It's

not natural. Yer hands, arms and face, well that's different, isn't it? They've got to poke out, haven't they?'

In the 1960s Sam would guard his boat against hippies sleeping in it. Many a young man about to kip in the boat had been scared witless by a hollering Sam emerging apparently from the ground with a torch under his chin.

'Well,' continued Mike, 'he was drunk as a lord. Warbling about bloody funny fish and how he was going to catch his own from then on. I asked him who the bloke was Miss Baker sent. And he laughed. "Bloody funny bloke," he said. "Click, click, mind your head, Sam. Brought a flask and sandwiches. Nice sandwiches." I couldn't get any more sense out of him. I had to go, Father. At that time I still found drunkenness upsetting, especially when it was Sam.'

A tear ran down Mike's face. 'I wish I'd stayed now. I miss him.'

Father Peter was comforting the old seaman when he suddenly remembered the jottings in red ink that Bessie had added in her diary.

'Wasn't Miss Baker worried about some men she'd seen at the funeral?' he asked tentatively.

'There was only Miss Baker, Jenny Allan and myself at the service, Father. I think it was Mrs Allan who saw some blokes in a car and wondered if they were Sam's friends. I didn't think they were. She went over to them but they told her they were waiting for the next funeral.'

'Did Miss Baker say anything to you about them?'

'Funny you should say that.' Mike paused and chewed the inside of his cheek. 'Yeh, now you remind me, that's when Miss Baker got a bit worried. I think she thought they might be police. She said to me, "Mike, don't mention anything about what Sam told you."'

He gave a deep sigh. 'I've broken my promise haven't I? But I don't expect she'd mind now.'

Father Peter was searching for the appropriate reassuring

56

words, when Mike suddenly said, 'It makes me think, though, Father. The night he was supposed to have drowned – well, it was a fine night. At the inquest they just presumed he must have been drunk and lost his footing. Death by misadventure.' He shook his head. 'I've seen Sam drunk in a gale and he's never lost his balance.'

When Father Peter left the launderette, he continued to walk northwards, in a clumsy attempt to convince Mike, if he was watching, that he was indeed on his way to visit someone. He hated the subterfuge, especially with Mike. It seemed so dishonest. When he was safely out of sight of the launderette he turned left and headed back through Saint Michael's Place and downhill towards Saint Mary Magdalene's.

The buildings in Saint Michael's Place were all painted and well managed now, or at least most of them were. Some of the occupants even owned the flats under the usual leasehold agreement. It was all so different from when he had first visited Bessie in 1952. There were cars now. People in those days were lucky to have a bicycle. Now there were attractive curtains or blinds at the windows and fancy pot plants. There was a mixture of Chinese, Sudanese, Indian, African and Irish, as well as the indigenous Brightonians living there.

A warmly clad young man came out of a front door to start defrosting his car windscreen. In 1952, Father Peter thought, most of the people were so poor they had hardly enough to buy a pair of shoes. When he used to visit Tad and Halina, smells of cooking wafted down the street, usually the aroma of various stews. It lingered in hallways, seeped from under doors and seemed to hang in the air day and night.

He walked gingerly in the middle of the road where tyre marks had flattened the snow and left odd patches of tarmac. He remembered having a conversation with Tad in the 1950s and being deeply shocked when Tad had told him about the corruption among the police. He hadn't wanted to believe it. They had argued, he accusing Tad of being cynical, Tad telling him that he didn't know what was going on in the town. Tad had been right. Peter had apologised to him when the trials began of the police officers involved. Then there were the trials in the early seventies of a group of policemen who were involved in burglaries. Again, Tad had known about it from his network of gossip among the traders and dealers. Tad had told him a joke when he was having dinner at the restaurant: 'It doesn't fall off the back of a lorry any more, Peter, but out of a police van.'

Tad would never let him pay when he went to the restaurant and would be really hurt if a fortnight passed without his putting in an appearance there. He would telephone and say, 'What's the matter, Peter – is my restaurant not good enough for you?'

When Cardinal Karol Wojtyla of Cracow became Pope John Paul II, Tad threw a great Polish party at the restaurant. The food was in abundance and chilled vodka, served in iced, salted glasses, flowed in a never-ending stream. Father Peter had never ever had such a hangover in his life. As he walked along the road, he chuckled at the memory of the green and yellow complexion he saw when shaving the next morning. The dreadful sight in the mirror had scared him into abstinence for at least a month.

He thought of Tad subdued, a ghastly white colour and very fearful after his first heart attack, when he knew Stella was missing in Africa. He was in hospital, in intensive care, and desperate to make his confession. Father Peter could see him clutching a picture of Saint Jude in his hand. 'I have cheated the tax, Father. I also used to serve pork as veal. It was just a question of bashing it . . .' The picture of Saint Jude was the one in the Filofax. Of course, Bessie was with him when he died; she must have kept it.

Why had the police not found the murderer yet? Father

Peter wondered. Years had passed since the deaths. Perhaps they still suspected him. He shivered at the thought. It was possible. After all, they had suspected him once.

As he started the walk down the steeper part of the hill, the road became more treacherous. Common sense told him not to risk a fall, so he carefully slid over to the tall ironwork railings, and, holding tightly, eased his way down the slippery pavement.

As he drew near to Maureen's home he could see Jack Evans clearing the snow from his front pathway. Jack's face was red with the cold.

'Hello, Father. You be careful. Are you OK or do you want some help?'

Father Peter draped himself over their gate. 'I'm perfectly all right, thank you, Jack.' The indignity of old age made him rage inside. As a marine he had run down rough ice-covered hills steeper than this. He had been well built and tough. Now he felt as delicate as some cheaply made birdcage – one fall and the inevitable break would occur, and he would end up like so many of his parishioners: in bed in plaster.

'I was just talking to someone about the gale of eighty-seven, and we were remembering your chimney coming down,' he said, trying to sound in control. If the Boss had presented Jack to him, it was his duty to forget his discomfort and try to pursue his enquiries.

Jack Evans looked at him and became silent. His shoulders drooped and his mouth seemed to thin suddenly, forcing his normally strong jawline into a sagging, pouched look of sadness and despondency. For a moment he looked much older than his forty-seven years. He sighed, and then quickly regained a more cheerful composure and came over to him.

'I'm not a superstitious man, Father, but that storm was like the beginning of a curse on us. The damage to the house, trying desperately to find some scaffolding, and a builder

59

free at the time who could start work straight away so we could protect the rest of the roof and the rooms underneath the gaping hole from all the rain and wind. I mean, Father, half the roof had gone. Do you remember?'

'I most certainly do,' Father Peter replied. 'You had the most horrendous damage. I do remember quite clearly.'

'Well,' Jack went on, 'we got the best quote we could at the time. Then came the fight with the insurance company over the bills. They said we hadn't shown them a cheaper quote. But the fellow who really quoted the cheapest price was a cowboy. We didn't trust him. The insurance company just didn't want to pay, Father. Well, I suppose they took a hammering after the gales. All the years they just collect, don't they? Then everyone claims at the same time. So then came the court case – of course we lost. Who can take on those big city boys? Especially the insurance companies. The court case was a joke. The stuffed shirt of a judge was obviously friendly with the insurance company's QC. They even joked together. Our barrister didn't get a look in. We were utterly carved up by a blatantly prejudiced judge. Our barrister said we could appeal on a point of law. We couldn't get the judgement overturned though because the judge, when he knew we might appeal, checked the transcript and made sure he worded his summing up really carefully. What's the point of a point of law, I said, if we can't overturn that creep's decision. Justice!'

He threw his head back as if appealing to the heavens. Then he laughed.

'We didn't have the money to appeal in any case. We also realised our bank was tied up with the insurance company. Honestly, Father, it was like waking up to find out that the world you thought you were living in had never existed.'

He grinned ruefully. 'And then there were the terrible murders and those telephone calls. We didn't know if the calls were the insurance company's private detectives, trying to unhinge us before the case – they *had* employed them to check up on us, honestly; they even looked into our bank accounts. As I said, we didn't know if it was them or some petty villain down here, or what. All I know is we aged those three years. We got ill, my work started to dry up as funding for theatres was cut. I don't know what kept Maureen going – she's so tough – but it has taken its toll. Our luck didn't change until she took a mad risk in Nice.'

Father Peter tried to calm Jack's bitterness. 'I haven't seen Maureen for some time now,' he said.

'Usually she's so tired, Father, she tries to rest on Saturdays. I think she's starting this funny change-of-life thing. She's got an afternoon free on Thursday, something or other's happening at the university, so why don't you come for tea? I'm sure she'd love to see you.'

'I've got two funerals on Thursday, but I should be free by teatime.'

'Good. We'll see you then.'

'Definitely.' He released his grip on the gate and was about to continue his journey downhill, when he remembered to ask Jack what he meant when he referred to 'those telephone calls'.

'Sorry, Father, I presumed you knew, but of course it was only the other magistrates who knew. It was after Bessie had her robbery. There were endless nuisance calls. They all had them.'

'Really?' Father Peter replied. 'I didn't know. Well, I'll see you on Thursday Jack. My regards to Maureen.'

It was almost a meditative experience. With each mouthful of hot leek-and-potato soup, he could feel the different sections of his body warming, bit by bit, one at a time. Not even the fact that Stella had returned his call and was going to telephone back at five-thirty could take his attention from the visceral sensuality of the soup.

61

The effect of soup, subterfuge and ordained skulduggery had exhausted him. His brain was shutting off all the reasoning faculties and demanding sleep. Stomach distended after the main course of toad-in-the hole, followed by sweet apple pie, and having set his alarm clock, he fell on to his bed hoping for a fifteen-minute nap.

He dreamed of a childhood summer. He could hear her singing against the rhythmic sounds of butter being patted into shape. And she was there, he could see her, could smell the warmth of her blonde hair caught back at the neck. There were the scents of newly mown grass, salt breezes on the Hunstanton beach, the tang of shrimp nets drying in the sun, and the sweet taste of homemade jam. He could feel her warm skin, as smooth as the eggs she gently lifted from beneath the complaining hens. Her face was perfumed from the lavender soap and face powder, and throughout the house there was the heady aroma of burnt sugar before she pounded her homemade stickjaw toffee out of the roasting-tin and on to the scrubbed wooden kitchen table. The whole dream was a collage of sweet gentleness.

'Red sky at night is the shepherd's delight. Red sky in the morning is the shepherd's warning.' He could hear his mother's Norfolk lilt, could feel her soft arms and the scrunching pleasure of touching the freshly laundered puffed sleeves on her new summer dress. 'A swarm of bees in May is worth a load of hay. A swarm of bees in June is worth a silver spoon.' He was shivering with awe thinking about the mysteries of God and Nature. They were gazing together at an angry morning sky.

And then the sky was turning green. And a bell was ringing. Old Sam was shouting at him from a boat out at sea. He drifted away from his mother towards Sam and saw he was shaking a handbell.

'I'll do you a favour, Peter,' Sam shouted. 'Time to go to

school, time to learn about anger. Fear is anger, Peter. Anger is fear.'

He woke up. The school bell was calling the children in from the playground.

Stella telephoned promptly at five-thirty. She apologised for not getting in touch with him before Monday but explained about her problems with the time change and how she had a deadline for Wednesday. She chatted for a while about the Caribbean and then asked him whether he had told anyone else about the Filofax.

'No one, Stella, just you. Why, do you think I should go to the police?'

'No, don't,' she replied, 'not yet, don't tell anyone. Wait until I've had time to think.'

'Will you help me?'

'Of course I will, but I'm tied up until Wednesday. After I get the feature out of the way . . . Look, why don't you come for lunch on Thursday? Are you free then?'

Everyone wanted him on Thursday, he thought with amusement. 'I can't manage Thursday,' he replied, 'but what about Friday?'

'I'll be in Prague.'

He groaned.

'But only for the day,' she said quickly. 'What about next Monday? Lunch? I'll make some pasta.'

He checked his diary. 'Yes, that will be fine. What time shall I come?'

'Come about twelve-thirty. I should be finished my piece by Saturday night. So by Monday I can give all my attention to the Filofax. Don't forget to bring it, will you?'

'No – I'll see you Monday.'

Stella was being very casual about the Filofax, Father Peter thought sadly. It was when Stella was over-casual, too bright

63

or sarcastically witty that she was usually covering up her pain, her real emotions. The only time she had been unable to do this – and he had seen her totally distraught – was at Bessie's funeral. When she had come back from Africa after her unspeakable experiences in the jail, she had been casual or she had made wisecracks about recommending the place as a slimming-farm. She had been the same when she was a child. If she fell over, the chin would jut forward, the teeth would clench and, even if tears were welling up in her eyes, she would say, 'Of *course* it didn't hurt. I'm all right.'

He decided that he would have to be careful when he talked to her about the diary. He did not want her reliving the anguish of that terrible summer.

By nine-thirty that evening the temperature was a little higher. Then the rain came. It fell heavily, pounding the snow into a grey slush. Father Peter sat at his desk watching the grey rivulets running down his bedroom window. He had his notebook and Bessie's Filofax, and was trying to make sense of what he'd learned that day.

It was possible that there had been four murders. If Sam had indeed been murdered, as Bessie and Mike suspected, could the other three all be connected with what Bessie had found out about the fishing trips? And was there any link with the nuisance calls? Who was the man Bessie trusted to go with Sam? He searched for inspiration but it was no good. Perhaps he should go down to the Marina and see if the Boss wanted to give him some more clues. The thought depressed him. It was the last place he wanted to visit. It would bring back the nightmare of Bank Holiday Monday, the twenty-seventh of August, three days after Bessie's funeral.

He had been sitting at his desk as he was now, but it was seven o'clock in the evening and a thick sea mist had descended on Brighton. He had been writing the weekly newsletter and listening to the sound of the foghorn, when the telephone had rung. It was Jenny and she was crying.

'I've done something very silly, Father,' she said. 'I've been very wicked.'

'Where are you Jenny? At home?'

'No, Father, I'm on *Jester*. We're moored to the main jetty. The mist will be gone tomorrow morning and we're setting off for Nice.' She began to snivel.

'Is Robert with you?'

'No, he's coming down later. I had to bring some things, so I came down early.'

'Are the crew with you?'

'No, they've got everything ready and they've gone ashore. Chef's left me some salad niçoise.'

'I'm sure you haven't done anything really wicked Jenny – you're not capable of it.'

'I am, Father.' There was a wail and sobbing. 'I want to make a confession, Father, in case I die.'

He became very worried. Were there marriage difficulties? Had Bessie's murder frightened her?

'I'll come down straight away Jenny. Make yourself some tea, and I'll be down as soon as I can get there.'

Father Peter remembered the concern he felt for her as he telephoned for a taxi and then tried to reach Robert. Robert's phone was engaged and the taxi took half an hour to arrive. The fog, along with the carbon monoxide fumes from the heavy traffic, slowed his journey so that it took much longer than he had hoped. It was eight o'clock by the time he arrived at the entrance to the harbour and he could not see further than fifteen feet ahead of him.

Jester was a two-hundred-and-ten-ton motor yacht. Its length was a hundred and eleven feet. After he passed the harbour office he turned left and made his way carefully along a floating pontoon in the direction of *Jester*'s haze of lights. As he walked he heard the sound of the foghorn on the arm of the Marina and the rumble of unseen traffic on the main coast road. The strange fluting sounds of moving metal, combined with his tentative efforts to keep his balance as he walked along the pontoon, created a feeling of separation from the world. His sense of detachment increased when a sudden movement of the boat caused *Jester*'s gangway to creak and groan.

Once aboard, he made his way to the aft deck and the double doors of the saloon area. He saw her lying on an easy chair close to one of the large windows. Her skirt was draped so that a beautiful, smooth leg was exposed. She was wearing one of her favourite silk blouses, with the buttons undone to the brassiere, and he could see the mound of her breast.

And then he felt the erection. He tried to stop it. He called her name and coughed. His voice had become husky with passion. All he wanted to do was to rush in and take her in his arms. She seemed not to hear. He walked through the doors thinking she was asleep. He was glad that she wasn't upset any more, and a part of him hoped she wouldn't wake until he'd had the chance of just touching the beautiful blonde hair.

Then he'd noticed that her head was in a funny position. It was too far round to be comfortable enough to sleep. He touched the beautiful head and it lolled forward. Brushing back her hair, he saw that her face had become almost ruddy in colour, not at all like her usual peaches-and-cream complexion. Her staring eyes were bloodshot.

He realised that she was dead. Her neck had been broken. The shock, and the fact that his damned erection still had not gone down, made him scream with anguish. He felt his mind divide into compartments, becoming a kaleidoscope of separate thinking areas, while he babbled and screamed that another one he loved had been taken. He relived being twelve years old, and screaming at God on the Hunstanton beach.

He ran along the companionway and reached the stairway

to the bridge wing, but realised he didn't know how to work any of the equipment. His eyes were blurred from crying and he was panicking. He returned to the saloon, half hoping that she was alive and playing tricks. Her lifeless body was still there. He ran out, up the stairway to the boat deck and screamed for help. All he could see was mist and all he could hear were the echoing screams of seagulls.

He remembered falling as he ran back along the pontoon shouting for help. A young police constable with *Jester*'s engineer picked him up. By then he was babbling incoherently about Jenny's neck being broken. The constable had run to the yacht while he seemed to be walking forever in mist, until he was suddenly by the harbour office, and two police officers were helping him to a police car where they said he could sit with them. One of the compartments of his mind, disgusted that he should have had an erection, was confessing to the sin of lust. Another part of his brain was lost in a whirling darkness of despair. The policemen were kind.

'What are you sorry for Father?'

And he had told them about lust and what it can do. And how he felt ashamed for what had happened. He had felt the same way, he told them, when his mother had told him not to bounce a beachball in the kitchen. And he had, and it had landed in a bowl of Yorkshire pudding. He had felt ashamed, he told them, because she got cross and threw it into the garden. Leaves and gravel stuck to the bright bouncing thing, removing its magic quality and reducing it to a rolling, sticky, chaotic mess.

'Are you saying you're responsible for this?' one of the policemen asked. And another part of his mind began a theological discussion about guilt. More police cars arrived. And an ambulance. He had hoped that perhaps with the miracles of medicine they might be able to bring her back to life, but they were suggesting that he should go with them to the police station where he could help them by answering some more questions.

What he said to them was still ingrained in his memory. He had read his own signed statement so many times. No wonder they suspected him – they had reasonable grounds for doing so. What he had said to the police was like the ravings of a lunatic. He had no idea shock could affect the mind so dramatically.

He was taken to the station, where he walked though cream-painted corridors which reminded him of a hospital. He was shown into a stark, sparsely furnished room, given a very old chair to sit on, next to a blue-lined metal table which was secured to the floor. The young police constable who had taken him there never said a word to him but just let him ramble on about the various aspects of reality.

Two CID men in suits came into the room, introduced themselves and started to ask him who owned the boat and how long he had known the owners. He had replied that Jenny was one of his girls. Who were the others? they asked him, and he had told them that Mike called Bessie, Maureen, Stella and Jenny Father Peter's girls.

'Is Bessie, Miss Baker?' one of them asked.

'Yes.'

'Did you ever visit Miss Baker at her home?'

'Oh yes, often.'

'Why did Mrs Allan ask you to come to the boat?'

'Because she wanted to make a confession before she left for Nice.'

'What did she say she'd done?'

'She didn't tell me, but even if she had I couldn't as a priest possibly tell you that,' he replied.

Then the police constable returned with a cup of tea. It was very sweet tea. He remembered sipping it slowly and trying to pull some of the different parts of his brain together.

One of the CID men left. The remaining man was very softly spoken and asked him gently how long he had been a priest. He seemed to be quite a religious man, Father Peter thought. He remembered asking him whether he was a Catholic, to which the man replied that he too had been brought up by the Jesuits.

'You're obviously distressed about Mrs Allan, Father Peter. Would you like to tell me how much she meant to you?'

How much she had meant to him? How could he begin to tell him how much she had meant to him? He had been overcome by a convulsion of deep sobbing.

'I realise how traumatic this is for you, Father.' The detective had been so gentle and understanding, almost like another priest.

And then all his feelings from the past had poured out. Words tumbling one after another. He was saying things he had never before realised about himself. He told him how Jenny had always been his favourite child, described how she would skip up to him and look up with those large innocent eyes. Her dear little ways. Her worries: 'Oh Father, I pulled out one of Mummy's flowers by mistake – I thought it was a weed.' What a beautiful young girl she'd become.

And then the horror when at the age of forty-two, having never ever been confronted with lust, he had gazed down at her beautiful young breasts heaving against her cotton dress as she knelt for the communion and had the most terrible erection. He had felt so guilty. She'd been only a child of fifteen. It was 1967 and she was wearing a miniskirt. Every time he saw her in the street, her beautiful young legs would start off another wave of lust. He told how he had dreamed and imagined lustful thoughts and tried to avoid her.

'Did you have the same lustful thoughts about Miss Baker?'

'Gracious, no. She was a dear girl, and very pretty, but no – Bessie never seemed to bring out the Old Nick syndrome.'

'Why do you think Mrs Allan brought it out in you, Father? And why again this summer?'

He had racked his brains to find the answer. All the different compartments of thinking were throwing up conflicting answers. One part of him said it was the heat, another part said it was the silk blouses she wore slightly opened at the neck. It was the smell of her perfume as she passed by, the blonde hair she sometimes caught at the nape of her neck. And some strange part of his brain and memory bank threw up an answer that suprised him as he sat talking to the CID man. 'Because she's like my mother,' he found himself saying. And he had cried again. 'And mother was taken in the summer by Him.'

'By who, Father?'

'The Boss. She had the same fair hair as mother. She smelt the same, she had the same smile, the same laugh, the same neckline.'

And he had disappeared into a silent world of thought, travelled through corridors of memories, searching for all the moments of truth and the reasons why his vulnerabilities had made him susceptible to Old Nick.

The detective had got up from the table and walked out of the room.

Two of them had returned but he was still locked into his own thoughts. Through what seemed like water he heard one of them say, 'Father Peter, the body of a lady who we know to be Mrs Jennifer Sian Allan has been found earlier tonight, and in connection with her death I'm going to arrest you. You are not obliged to say anything unless you wish to do so but what you say will be taken down and may be given in evidence . . .'

70

Then he was going along more cream-coloured corridors to the security block and being given to someone called a custody sergeant. He was told the circumstances of his arrest and the new man said, 'I'm authorising your detention to secure further evidence. Do you want a solicitor?'

He was too locked into his own mind to care.

'No,' he said.

'You are going to have a duty solicitor then,' the custody officer replied.

A charming man arrived and told him he was the solicitor brought in to help him. Then they were taking his clothes and giving him a sealed packet containing some white overalls to wear. They were taking samples from his hair and nails and taking fingerprints. He was led along to the cells with the duty solicitor saying all the time, 'If you're innocent, Father, you've nothing to fear.' To which he replied, 'Fear is a terrible thing if one does not have faith.'

They were taking another man into the cells. There was a struggle and he heard the cell door slam shut. It was a dreadful sound. He was taken courteously to his own cell, where there was a hard wooden bunk on which he expected he would sit and sleep. It was covered by a thin, blue, plastic-coated rubber mattress. He waited for the door to slam but instead they left it open, and a young policeman sat on a chair nearby and read a newspaper, glancing towards him every so often.

'How long will I be here?' Father Peter had asked him.

'Just until they've received the forensic reports back from Aldermaston.'

'How long will that be?'

'Can be up to seventy-two hours.'

During those hours spent in the police cell, he had sifted

through, meditated and contemplated on his own truths. He had never found the reason for his first confrontation with lust when it had taken him in 1967. Sitting in the lonely cell, having turned all the questions over to the Boss, he was given the answer. He had known it all along but not wanted to face up to it.

He had always accepted what his father had told him about his mother's death. 'Because she was perfect, God took her.' After his twelfth year, the memory of his mother gradually merged with the image of the Virgin Mary. She remained forever perfect, dressed in blue and lit by the flickering light of a candle. Up until the age of seventeen he had gone out with girls, been attracted to them, as had every other young lad. At twenty he returned home after the war, a hardened marine.

He had gone down to the beach with Tom, the only one of five brothers who had survived the war. (He had been in ground control in the RAF.) He had asked his older brother about the body. He could never remember there ever having been a body or a funeral. 'Why wasn't I taken to Mother's funeral?'

Tom had walked in silence for a while, then said, 'We were told not to tell you, Peter. You were the baby and very close to her. But I can tell you now. She didn't die. She ran off and left Dad for a fellow in Norwich. Dad was heartbroken.'

They had continued walking in silence while Peter tried to rearrange eight years of delusion.

'Is she still alive?'

'I think so.'

Without telling their father, they went looking for her. They found her serving in a pub owned by the man with whom she lived. She was wearing bright red lipstick, had a coarse loud laugh, and she was fat.

'Let's get out of here,' Tom said. He had dragged Peter

out of the bar. The two of them had gone round the corner of the pub and cried like children.

It was from that day on that Peter had felt no attraction for women. It was as if something had died. During his priest's training he accepted it as a blessing. The raging lust that returned in 1967 when he was forty-two was sparked off, he now realised, by Jenny's resemblance to his mother, as he had known her as a child. Perfect again. Clean, wholesome, innocent, a beautiful woman.

He had been in the cell for forty-eight hours when the CID asked him some different questions.

They wanted to know whether he knew Charles Nightingale. And whether he too was a member of his church.

He had told them that Charles's family always attended but Charles usually came only at Easter and Christmas.

His solicitor told him that Nightingale had been found on the Downs, at Devil's Dyke, shot through the head. He also said that Jenny's husband, Robert Allan, had informed the police that the safe on board *Jester* had been robbed of a large amount of money.

After the news of the missing money, and then the negative results of the forensic tests, all charges against him were dropped. When Father Peter was released from police custody, he returned to a welcome-home party at Saint Mary Magdalene's. His flock took back their sad shepherd. They gathered him to their hearts, and he had felt so proud and grateful for their absolute trust in his innocence.

Stella had been there. She hugged him, and there were tears in her eyes as she said, 'You shouldn't hang about in jails, Father. It wasn't too bad for you, was it? I prayed for you.'

He had been just another mourner at Jenny's funeral. After discussions with the bishop, it was agreed that even though Robert Allan wished him to take the service it would be politically unwise to do so. It would have given the predatory media a field day.

It had been late autumn when the leaves on the trees were a golden brown, that Charles Nightingale's family loyally insisted that he take the Requiem Mass for them, and they had been through the awful stress of having to wait for a month before Charles's body could be released by the coroner.

It had been one of the biggest funerals Brighton had ever known. After the mass, Father Peter had ridden in the hearse, sitting behind Barry, the funeral director, and the driver.

Now, he gripped the Filofax again with excitement. Why hadn't he thought of it before? Of course, Barry was the duty funeral director the night of Charles's murder. He was going to be in charge of both funerals on Thursday. Father Peter wrote down in his notebook some questions that he hoped Barry would be able to answer.

He looked back at the Filofax. In a section of blue pages at the back of the diary, Bessie had written some of her philosophical thoughts. He thumbed through the pages. There were notes on Benjamin Franklin's *Virtues*, on *Intercession* by Dr Reinhold Niebuhr. There was a page on *Gratitude* from Saint Augustine, and Bessie's attempts at writing some poetry, entitled *After the Fines Court*.

He reached the end of the blue pages and noticed there was a wallet inside the black leather cover. He felt inside and drew out a small photograph. It was one of a strip of pictures taken in a passport booth. It showed a smiling Bessie, holding a baby in her arms. In her left hand, facing the camera was a soft toy dog with a patch over his eye. Father Peter had bought it from a collection of homemade toys at a local Red Cross bazaar during the summer of 1973, when everyone thought Bessie was away attending trade union studies. He had given it to her when he visited her in the London hospital. He tried to persuade her to keep the child. But she wanted the boy to have a better chance in life with two parents. Many a time she'd wept on his shoulder, wondering whether she had done the right thing.

4

It had been a successful day, Stella thought, as she checked
the indicator board at Victoria Station. She had delivered the
Grenada feature on time, been booked for two really good
travel assignments, had the promise of a possible chance to
be put forward for a correspondent's job, and had even been
able to move her dental appointment forward to fit in with
all her other business, thanks to someone being snowbound
in Kent.

She had five minutes to walk briskly to platform nineteen
for the Brighton train. She stepped carefully. The strange
white surface on the station's platform could sometimes be
slippery if one was wearing leather soles – and she was a
little squiffy from all the brandy and wine.

She had enjoyed the party. It was a send-off for Colin's
friend Mike, who was being moved from being the BBC's
correspondent in Bosnia, to being Moscow correspondent.

The party was held at the Langham Hilton, opposite
Broadcasting House. She had seen people she hadn't met
up with since her times in Africa, and been gratified by
their apparent delight at meeting her again. 'Stella – my
God, fancy seeing you. I was only talking about you the
other day . . .'

From seven-thirty onwards they had drifted in and out of
the bar, reporters from the old Fleet Street days, greeting her
with great yelps of real pleasure. One of the journalists from

the *Telegraph* told her about a correspondent's job going in Warsaw. He promised to find out whether the position was already filled and, if not, put her name forward to the editor. She had felt the buzz again, been one of the gang of world voyeurs with their familiar jocularity, fast political quips, rehashed old stories and gossip.

She found, to her surprise, that she was now able to joke about the African prison experience and feel no inner pain. It had been the same with all the other dramas in her life. Perhaps it was because she had been in the company of others like herself, journalists who could momentarily detach themselves emotionally from the story they were reporting, paying for that detachment later, in dreams. She had enjoyed being with them again. She would still be with them now if she didn't have to be up so early in the morning to get the flight to Prague.

Colin had been there, back on leave from Hong Kong. When she first caught sight of him she panicked, until it slowly dawned on her that she was able to talk to him as just another friend. The ten years' separation had healed the pain she thought would never leave her. Just occasionally, the way he held his head or moved his mouth would bring back the memory of how she had once felt, but his changed physical appearance (he had developed a small paunch and his hairline had receded) reminded her of the fact that he had always been much older than she was.

She had not noticed it in her late twenties and early thirties, and when he left her he had been forty-two, in his prime. Now he was in his fifties, while she was still a young-looking forty-three. He had looked at her appreciatively and complimented her on her healthy tan. There was the beginning of a flirtatious twinkle in his eye. She heard a little voice inside her head say, 'Dream on, Colin; you blew it and I'm not into married men.' But she had said, charmingly, 'And you look very affluent and successful.'

She found an empty compartment, flopped into the window seat and inspected all her packages. She had bought some new shorts and a couple of T-shirts for her cruise in March and had been given some smart combinations from a fashion house.

The new popular way of holiday travel was now a cruise, according to the women's magazine editor. Everyone was wanting to cruise, not just the over-fifties but the young, especially in America, and Stella's job was to compare the American luxury experience with the British *QE2*.

'I'm going to need some clothes,' she complained. 'I don't usually wear lots of formal dresses and glitzy numbers.' She was packed off to the fashion department who arranged some deal with a designer to let her wear his clothes as long as she mentioned his name in the article. 'Can I keep the clothes afterwards?' she asked. He had grudgingly agreed that she could.

The carriage door slid open and a weary-looking commuter settled into the opposite corner of the compartment. Within minutes he was snoring fitfully, his chin buried deep in his striped businessman's shirt. Stella felt sorry for him. He was obviously exhausted. She relaxed back into her own seat, waiting for the train to depart and reliving moments from the party.

'You're very brown,' an attractive male voice said. 'I don't call you Ma'm now, do I? It's Ms Potocki, isn't it?' Stella searched her memory. She knew his face. He was tall, about forty, with grey green eyes and a cheerful, slightly cheeky smile. It was the dark mole on his cheek that jogged her memory. She remembered seeing it when she had signed her first warrant, and an unshaven, scruffy, long-haired, disreputable-looking character in filthy jeans had stood before her and had sworn on the bible that he was a police officer. She remembered thinking that the beauty spot could have placed him in a restoration play as a villain who was really the son of a lord.

'Hello.' She looked quickly towards the now heavily snoring man in the corner. 'Are you on duty? I don't want to break your cover.'

He grinned. 'No, finished for the day.' He sat down opposite her. 'So, have you been on holiday?'

She told him about the feature on the Caribbean and he groaned with mock envy. 'It's all right for some.'

The train started to pull out of Victoria.

'I'm right, you're not a magistrate any more are you?'

'No, I had to be away too much with my work.' Stella chose her words carefully. She did not want to ruin her mellow mood with a tirade about the lack of respect she had for the judicial system. She changed the subject. 'The last time I saw you was at the lecture at Lewes, in the late eighties when you and I had a row about journalists, do you remember?'

He laughed. 'Oh I do remember. I was new to giving talks to magistrates and I was trying to keep it light – you know, make a joke. I didn't think I had a journalist sitting out there. And then, wham bam, you really had a go. Next thing we're into police corruption, the lot. And I thought the biggest excitement was going to be when I showed them a block of cannabis.'

Stella smiled wickedly. 'I meant every word. Are you still lecturing or are you back in the field.'

'I've been moved up.'

'Congratulations. To what?'

'Assistant Chief Constable – Crime and Operations.'

'I'm very impressed.' The need to tease him was overwhelming. 'Is that because of your freemasonry contacts or your brilliant work?'

He leant his head back against the covered headrest and grinned at her. 'Oh my, you really are suspicious of policemen.'

'You bet.'

'What happened? Did a cop leave you in the middle of the road when you were little and tell you to play with the traffic?'

Stella laughed and looked out of the window. Clear red, amber, green and sparkling diamond-white lights winked like jewels among London's passing black geometric shapes. Behind the buildings, heavy purple clouds crossed the dark winter sky. She looked back at him. His head was turned in the direction of the other passenger who was now shaking with great rattling snores, but he was still watching her out of the corner of his eye.

He smiled. 'I was lucky enough to be in the office when a packet of photographs arrived which led the squad to the biggest drug bust the country had ever seen. Being associated with it helped me come to the notice of the big brass.'

'That was a lucky break,'

'It was – if I knew who sent them I'd buy them a drink. So, where are you off to next?'

'Prague.'

'It's a beautiful city. I was there about a year ago on the trail of a villain.'

'I was there before the wall came down, when I was covering more serious things than holidays.'

'Arms?'

'Yes, I had to track down some of the PLO training there. The worst moment for me was entering from the Austrian border and being stopped and searched. They took away some German tabloids lying around in the car and missed all the other stuff.'

'I suppose in many ways our work is similar.'

'Sometimes we both have to appear to be something we're not to try to get at the truth, I suppose.'

He ignored the jibe. 'And after Prague where?'

'I'm going on a cruise in the Bahamas – Nassau, Coco

Cay – to see how the Americans do it. Then I have a couple of days in Miami before I leave on the *QE2* to see how the Brits serve up *their* cruises.'

'Can you take your own private detective?' he said, his eyes twinkling.

'Oh I think I can look after myself.'

The train pulled into East Croydon and a lad with a Sony Walkman tuned high enough for her to hear the rhythm of the cymbals sat beside her.

'Do you like ships? You don't get sea sick do you?'

'No I don't. I love ships.'

'Have you done a lot of sailing?'

'Not a lot. You?'

'I used to go fishing with my dad, off the coast at Littlehampton. Once a year the black bream would come up there to spawn and we would wait for them on their way back. Do you like fishing?'

'I've only ever fished from a friend's motor yacht, in the Mediterranean. I caught a sardine.'

'I used to go a lot as a boy.'

She wanted to know more about him. His eyes were giving her the come-on signs. If a tanned complexion had this effect on men, she thought, perhaps she should buy herself a sun lamp.

'Do you take your children fishing?' she asked.

'When I get the chance.' He had to be married, Stella thought. 'I sometimes have them for holidays.'

'Oh.'

'I'm divorced.'

'Sorry.'

'You never married?' he asked.

'No.'

'By choice? I must say I'm surprised, or am I being politically incorrect. Perhaps you never wanted to tie yourself up.'

What was he implying? Stella wondered. 'I had a long-term relationship with someone, and it didn't work out,' she said. 'A man not a woman. I'm not a lesbian.'

He roared with laughter. The snoring businessman woke with a start, looked out of the window, then sank gratefully back into his seat to begin another bout of noisy sleep.

'I never thought for a moment you were.'

Having stared at the luggage rack for the entire journey, despite nodding his head all the time, the lad with the Sony Walkman got out at Haywards Heath.

'Have you eaten?' he asked her.

'Lots of lovely canapés, thank you, and too much brandy and wine.'

'I was going to ask you if you'd like to come and have some Italian food with me when we get into Brighton.'

'Tonight I can't. I'm up too early in the morning to get the flight to Prague.'

'You're going tomorrow?'

'Yes, but I do love Italian food.'

'Would you like to come out another evening?'

'It would help if I knew your name.'

'I'm sorry, John Smith.' He searched his pocket and handed her a card.

Stella giggled. 'You're joking.'

'I'm not. It's very embarrassing when booking into a hotel.'

'I'll bet.'

'I use another name when I'm working, otherwise it becomes too suspicious.'

He had an attractive smile, Stella thought, and a good sense of humour. 'I'm in the phone book,' she said. 'Give me a ring.'

'I will.'

As the train pulled into Brighton station he asked whether she wanted a lift home.

'I have my own car. It's in the carpark,' she replied.

He insisted on walking to it with her. She was quite glad that he had offered. It was very cold, dark and badly lit in the station carpark. He took her arm and guided her through some slippery patches of ground. A fine sleet was falling. She could see the Saab at the far end of the carpark.

'Where's your car?' she asked. 'I don't want to take you out of your way.'

'It's over there,' he said pointing in the other direction.

A train-driver was getting out of a car near hers. He was an old friend of Bessie's. He saw Stella and waved.

'I'm OK now,' she said. 'Why don't you save yourself from getting wet?'

John released her arm. 'I'll ring you,' he said, then he turned and hurried back in the direction of the station.

'How are you keeping, Stella?' the train-driver asked.

'Fine, and you? Can't wait to get out of this awful weather.'

'You know your tax disc's out of date? Our Bessie would've smacked your hand for that,' he said.

As she drove home she started to laugh. I wonder if John Smith would have booked me, she wondered. Like a journalist, a policeman is never really off duty.

5

The second Requiem Mass was over. Father Peter waited outside the church until the last members of the grieving family were safely inside their chauffeur-driven cars, then he climbed into the hearse, and sat behind Barry, the funeral director, ready for the journey to the cemetery.

'Busy day today, Father?'

'Sadly yes.'

'I've got four Church of Englands tomorrow. All different churches. I'll be running around like a blue-arsed fly.'

At least Barry was in a talkative mood, Father Peter thought. Perhaps now was a good time to bring up the subject of Charles's murder.

He looked out of the window of the hearse, while he wondered how to phrase his questions. There were scattered patches of snow on the hillier areas of the town, while on the more sheltered ground, adding colour to the sombre earth, there were clumps of daffodils and hyacinths, opening their flowers to the warm spring sunshine.

'Barry?'

'Yes Father.'

'Do you remember Charles Nightingale's funeral?'

'Oh yes. There were cars going back nearly half a mile behind us then, weren't there. All those MPs and celebrities. Church was packed out wasn't it?'

'It certainly was.'

They travelled in silence for a while before Father Peter asked, 'Weren't you the duty funeral director the night he was murdered?'

'I was,' Barry replied, 'and a friend of mine, a chap who owns his own taxi, was the one who found him. He didn't work nights for ages afterwards.'

'How did he find him?'

'Well, this friend of mine, he's a teacher actually, drives the taxi to make a bit extra. Well, as I was saying, he got a booking that evening to pick up a John Smith at eleven o'clock on the dot from the pub at the Dyke. The fare is going to Gatwick, right, so my friend is really chuffed. So he's driving along Devil's Dyke Road, can see the pub, knows he's right on time. He's just approaching the pub, and can see a chap standing by the pub door watching as he drives up. So he says to himself, "This must be the Mr Smith for Gatwick." Then another bloke steps out of the shadow and is walking towards him, on the opposite side of the road from the pub.'

'So he could see two men in his headlights,' Father Peter interrupted.

'That's right, Father, two men. So, my friend is just wondering which one of them is the Mr Smith, when suddenly a car comes out of nowhere behind him. It must have been parked about fifty yards before you reach the Dyke. It comes right up to his back bumper, headlights full on. Then my friend hears what he thinks is a car backfiring. He pulls up beside a Jag he can see parked up ahead, at the end of the pub's carpark. By then the blokes from the car behind him have got out and are running towards the Jag. So are the other two, you know the one at the pub door and the one from the car park – all of them running towards the Jag. My friend walks towards the pub and shouts out to them as they pass him, 'Any of you a Mr Smith for Gatwick?' The four men pay no attention to him so my friend continues towards the pub door. Just as he's going in, he sees the two blokes from the car behind him get back in and tear off, and the other two get into another car, and they speed off as well. My friend thinks to himself, "Funny goings on," but he's concerned that he'll be late for his fare so he goes into the pub and asks for Mr Smith – no one. He says to the woman behind the bar, "But you ordered a cab for John Smith at eleven o'clock on the dot." "No I didn't," she says. So my friend goes out again, really fed up, because business is really bad, no one's taking taxis that evening and he thought he'd got one good fare.

'Anyway, he moves his car forward beside the Jag, reverses at a right angle, his lights full on the driver's door, when he realises there's something wrong. He gets out, goes towards the open driver's window, and sees Nightingale with his head blown to bits. So he goes running inside the pub again. The woman behind the bar says, "I've told you there's no Mr Smith." "Maybe," says my friend, "but there's a body in your carpark. You'd better call the police."

'Well, I was in my pyjamas and dressing-gown, watching a video with the wife. We'd had a takeaway Chinese. It had been a really relaxing evening. I was hoping I wouldn't be needed that night – that nobody would crash their cars – when the office puts through a call, and they tell me to go up and have a look at the body, to see if I can get the stretcher in.'

Barry gave a loud sigh, and paused for a second as if reliving the experience, then, emphasising every word he said, 'I tell you Father, after the police had finished and I looked inside the car, I could see there were bits of hair, blood, bone and brain splattered all over the passenger side. Not the best experience after a Chinese meal, I can tell you.'

Father Peter groaned. Barry had developed a macabre sense of humour to cope with the business of death. He often said, 'I'm offering two for the price of one this week, Father, business is slack.' Father Peter had heard the same kind of jokes from doctors dealing with incurable diseases. It was not callousness, just their way of coping with their daily, awful reality. One of his friends was a prison chaplain. He had developed a form of comedian's patter to cope with some of the evils he confronted in jail.

'I'm sorry, Father, has it upset you?' Barry was looking at him with concern.

'Yes, but no, please tell me everything, Barry, I want to know what happened.'

'You sure?'

'Yes.'

'Well we managed to get him on to the stretcher and we took him to the borough mortuary, labelled him and put him on to a tray for the fridge. There were powder burns on his forehead, where the bullet entered. It was a small entry wound from a nine-millimetre bullet, so I heard. I remember saying, who would believe such a small hole could have such a huge impact on the back of the head? He was shot right between the eyes. One of the scenes-of-crime boys told me he must have been looking right down the barrel when he was killed. He said the gun that had been used was a Luger.'

'A Luger?' Father Peter interjected.

'Yes,' Barry replied. 'That's what the police said. Anyway, when the post mortem was eventually over and the family contacted us, we had to advise them not to look at his head. There was nothing we could do to rebuild it or anything, it was too bad. So we covered his face and left his hand where they could touch it, for comfort. I felt sorry for his wife. She seemed a really nice woman. Right, Father, we're here.'

The hearse turned into the entrance gates of the cemetery, followed by the mourners' cars. Father Peter watched Barry carry the wreaths up to the graveside. Four men had been in the carpark the night Charles was killed. Were any of them the same men Bessie had seen at Sam's funeral?

After the burial ceremony was over, and he had spent some time comforting the more distraught members of the family, Father Peter got back into the hearse with Barry and the driver set off for Saint Mary Magdalene's.

'Did the police ever have a theory about Charles Nightingale's murder?' Father Peter asked.

Barry thought for a while. 'I think they said that what my friend thought was a car backfiring must have been the actual gunshot that killed him. So it couldn't have been the two men in the car behind him, or the two men he saw in his headlights. But what the four men were doing there they didn't know. They think someone must have got away down into the valley by one of the tracks.'

'A fifth man. He would have to be very fit,' Father Peter said. 'The valley's about three hundred feet down isn't it?'

'About that, I should think,' Barry replied.

'Did the police suspect anyone or know the reason for the murder?' Father Peter asked.

'No, I don't think so,' Barry replied. 'My friend was helping them for a long time though. They kept asking him to come in and look at mug shots. The police asked him if he thought they were Germans. I suppose because it was a Luger that shot him. But he said he thought they were English, probably Londoners, and they were bigger than your average height. They asked him what make of cars they were driving, but as my friend said he could only remember the Jag. The car behind him had blinded him with its headlights and he was too worried about being late for his fare to take more notice of the other car.'

The murderer would have to know the area very well to get away so quickly, Father Peter thought. The hearse pulled up outside the church.

'Did your friend ever find out who booked the taxi?' Father Peter asked as he got out.

'No,' Barry said. 'My friend always asks for the telephone number so he can ring back to confirm the booking. He rang back after the booking so he had the number, but when the police checked, it was a public phone box.'

'Do you know which phone box?'

'Yes, it was one of those behind the Albion, in the Steyne.'

Barry slid across his seat, wound down the window and touched Father Peter's arm. Lowering his voice he said, 'One thing I do know, Father, I've got a friend who knows someone in the CID, and apparently Nightingale's wife said he got a fax early that Tuesday morning, at home. Then he made lots of calls cancelling business meetings and told her he wouldn't be back until the early hours of Wednesday.'

'Did the police find the fax on him?' Father Peter asked.

'I don't know, Father.'

After he had changed his clothes, and before leaving the presbytery to visit Maureen, Father Peter took some time to add more relevant questions to his notebook.

Was the fax sent to Charles at his home from the murderer? Was the taxi booked for a Mr Smith anything to do with Charles's death? Who were the men in the other cars? And did Charles's murder have anything to do with what Bessie found out about the illegal fishing? Had the person who killed Charles also killed Sam, Bessie and Jenny?

'Better weather for you, Father?

Jack Evans led him into the warm, centrally heated hallway and helped him to take off his coat.

'It is indeed. It's quite warm out of the wind.'

'March has come in like a lamb; let's hope we have a good spring. Heaven knows, we need it after all this dreadful weather. Maureen's on the phone, then she's just got to fax a few things to the university. She won't be a minute. Go into the lounge and I'll bring in the tea.'

'I didn't know you had a fax machine,' Father Peter said. 'How long have you been using one of those?'

'Well, Father, even people who like the old ways have to catch up with modern technology. We got ours in the January sales, this year. It's cheaper than using the post.'

Father Peter sighed with relief. He liked Jack Evans. He was a kind, gentle man, and a very good husband for Maureen. He had always shared the chores and children's upbringing, and had a great respect and pride for all his wife's achievements. Whenever Father Peter saw them out walking together, they were always holding hands, and it gave him a profound sense of joy to experience again the great feeling of warmth and love in the house.

On the table in front of the fire were a selection of daintily cut sandwiches, small homemade scones with cream and jam, and a sponge cake. Maureen had always taken great care preparing a tea. Father Peter suddenly realised how much he had missed the cosy rituals that had stopped abruptly after Bessie's and Jenny's deaths.

He was eating his second sandwich and deeply engrossed in Jack's description of a new play he was thinking of directing, when she came into the room.

Maureen had lost weight. Her left eye had developed an occasional twitch and she swallowed nervously as she attempted to greet him with a smile. 'How lovely to see you Father. It's been too long.'

They exchanged pleasantries, talked about the children and problems at the university. She knew he was studying her and was aware that he was shocked by her appearance. Every so often a self-conscious flush crept up from her neck and into her cheeks. He knew that look. After all, he had known her as a young girl. Maureen had been a child incapable of telling a lie, who stuttered and flushed at even a half truth.

He waited until they had finished the cake and were more relaxed before saying, 'I hate to ask you, Maureen, because I know how much we all want to put the whole dreadful time behind us, but Jack was telling me about nuisance telephone calls after Bessie's robbery. When did they start?'

Her eyes hardened. 'I can tell you exactly,' she said. 'It was the Sunday night after the robbery. We had two calls, one at midnight and one in the early hours of the morning. After the second one I couldn't go back to sleep. I was in court on Monday morning and I felt terrible. Jack's told you about the problems that we were going through? Well I thought the whole world was against us. Then, when I got to court, I saw Charles as I came in through the door. He was talking to one of the other magistrates, a chap from British Telecom. I overheard Charles telling him about getting nuisance calls. I was just about to tell him about mine when I was called away by a clerk.

'I was so relieved, because Jack and I thought it was the insurance company up to their tricks – we were quite paranoid by then. So, ridiculous as it might sound, it was a relief to know other people were getting them. Then, after Bessie's murder, they stopped. I think Charles was probably the first one who knew who was making the calls because of his friendship with the chap from Telecom.'

'Did he tell you who it was?' Father Peter interrupted.

'No,' Maureen replied.

'Do you know the name of the Telecom man?'

'Yes.'

'Would he be able to tell us who was making the calls?'

Maureen gave a wry smile. 'I shouldn't think he would be allowed to, Father. I think only the police could tell you that. Nowadays, of course, there won't be so many nuisance calls with the new telephones that show the number dialling your phone.'

'It must have been very frightening for you at the time.'

'Yes it was.'

'Maureen, do you think that the calls were anything to do with the murders?'

Maureen frowned. 'What do you mean, Father? Are you wondering whether the person who made the calls was the murderer?'

'Yes.'

'No, Father it wasn't. The calls might have had something to do with Jenny's murder but they wouldn't have had anything to do with Bessie or Charles's death – I don't think.'

'How can you be so certain?'

Maureen sighed and looked across the room to Jack. 'I know who made the calls, Father.'

'You *do* know. Who?'

'Oh, Father, I feel awful telling you, but it was Jenny.'

'Jenny?' Father Peter felt as if he had been kicked in the stomach.

Maureen watched him cautiously. 'I'm sorry, Father. I know how much you cared for her, but Jenny was a very sick lady. She always wanted to be the centre of attention. She liked power. Power over other people. She would woo men and women, courting their friendship, flattering them. Nothing would be too much bother for her to do for you. Then she would find your Achilles heel. And she would use it mercilessly, to patronise and to look down on you. And you were a friend or equal no longer. She was like that as a child, manipulative, always wanting to create dramas.'

She laughed ruefully. 'I remember Stella giving her a terrible thumping when we were teenagers because Jenny had attended mass in a low-cut blouse, in an attempt to seduce you.'

Father Peter bit his lip until it hurt. Maureen mistook the

93

action for suppressed laughter. He was staring down at his hands so she couldn't see the pain he felt.

'Well, Father, you were the only glamorous man we little convent girls saw regularly. And we thought you were wonderful.'

'Maureen only went out with me, Father, because I was the closest resemblance to you she'd met,' Jack joked.

Father Peter was grateful for his intervention – it gave him time to recover.

'Well, I'm glad it was the girls who fancied me and not the boys,' he said. They roared with laughter.

'Would you like a drink, Father?' Jack asked. 'After all, it's not far off six.'

'Do you have any whisky?'

'I most certainly do,' Jack replied. 'It's what *I* drink. Maureen?'

'A gin and tonic, please.'

'How do you know for certain it was Jenny?' Father Peter said as Jack left to get the drinks.

'Because she told me herself, the night she was murdered,' Maureen replied, inspecting her thumbnail. Another flush crept round her neck. 'She telephoned me just after the Southern News – it must have been a little before seven – to say sorry. I think she felt responsible for Bessie's death in some way, because of her silly calls. She'd phoned Stella before calling me but Stella was out, and she'd called Charles on his mobile number. She said she was going to tell him that she was leaving for Nice and wanted to apologise for making the calls, and had just taken a breath, a pause, to sum up the courage to do it, when he said, "I know it's you Jenny." She was really upset because he sounded so angry.'

Maureen paused and seemed to choose her words very carefully.

'You see, Father, Charles and Jenny had a brief affair earlier that year. Bessie was very worried about it. She'd asked me whether we should have a word with her about the gossip. I told Bessie it was best not to interfere. Well, Jenny told me, that Charles said he knew she had been making the calls to his home, and she had made him very angry. She really was upset when she talked to me. She told me he said, "Been with any fishermen lately?" and had then switched off the mobile. She didn't understand what he meant. She asked me whether anyone had been gossiping about her having an affair with anyone. I told her that I hadn't heard anything.'

Father Peter was trying to divorce himself from his emotions and to hold on to every bit of information. Why, he wondered, had Charles asked Jenny about fishermen? Unless she had been seen at Sam's funeral by someone who told him. It still didn't make sense. As far as he knew it was only Mike, Sam and Bessie who knew about the possibility of the fishing quotas being broken. Unless the men in the car . . . ? Bessie had emphasised it in red ink. She had also warned Mike not to speak about anything. Perhaps it was something to do with the fishing quotas after all. But then why was Charles murdered? He felt totally confused.

Jack returned with the drinks. While Father Peter was sipping his whisky, he remembered that Bessie had written about how concerned she was that Maureen might lose her home.

'I'm glad you sorted out all your insurance problems,' he said. 'This is such a lovely house.'

'But we didn't, Father,' Jack said bitterly. 'They nearly ruined us. We would be homeless now if it hadn't been for Maureen's daring escapade.'

'What escapade?' Father Peter asked.

'Maureen, tell Father Peter about Nice.'

Maureen looked uncomfortable. She shrugged her shoulders and suggested that he would find it boring. Father Peter assured her that he would love to hear the story. Reluctantly she began, 'Well, we were all so upset and frightened after Charles was killed that a lot of us resigned from the bench. I was feeling ill with all the worry we'd been through and Stella was going on a trip to Rome for a magazine. She was supposed to have taken Bessie.' Maureen looked almost tearful for a moment as she said, 'What a good friend she was to me. She said I could go in Bessie's place and that it would do me good to get away, have a break from all our problems.' She sipped her gin and tonic thoughtfully. 'After we spent a week in Rome she suggested we go on to Nice. She paid all my expenses. She knew I had no money.'

Her cheeks began to redden and, in a distracted way, she loosened the top button of her blouse, and blew inside the material. Father Peter caught Jack's eye and realised that this was what he must have been referring to when he met him the other day. Maureen was having a hard time with the menopause.

Maureen continued with the story. 'When we got to Nice we had a mad night out and ended up in a casino – Ruhl's I think it was called. I've never gambled in my life, Father, but Stella said, "Go on let's see if we can change your luck." She lent me some money and I played roulette. And I just kept winning and winning until I knew I had enough to pay off our debts. Then I stopped.'

Her cheeks were scarlet as she finished the story. 'Isn't that a wonderful story Father?' Jack enthused. 'We were saved by a gamble. We were able to meet the legal costs and pay the bank what we owed them. I cried when she told me. She called me from Nice.'

'Remarkable,' Father Peter said. 'I didn't think anyone could really win in those places. I thought only the house won.'

'Well,' Maureen said, 'there was rather a large group of Australian tourists there. They were all middle-aged women. They came into the casino just behind us. I don't think they

96

intended to play. Stella thought the management let us win in order to attract them to the tables. If that's what their intention was, they certainly achieved their goal. All the women were playing by the time we left.'

'But Father,' Jack went on, 'one minute I thought we were completely ruined, the next we were saved by good fortune. At last we had found favour with the gods.' Jack shook his head with the wonderment of it all.

'Did you owe a lot of money Jack?'

'Did we owe a lot of money?' Jack laughed. 'Father, we owed the banks one hundred and twenty thousand pounds, didn't we Maureen?'

'Dear heavens, I had no idea you were in such financial trouble,' Father Peter exclaimed.

'No one did,' Jack said.

'The storm damage was seventy thousand, the rest was bank interest and legal costs. We used to feel time ticking past in pound notes, didn't we Maureen?'

'It must have been terrifying for you,' Father Peter said sympathetically.

'Of course it was,' Jack said. 'Can you imagine how we felt when Maureen came back from Nice with a cheque for one hundred and twenty-five thousand pounds?'

'Yes I can,' Father Peter murmured.

Maureen had finished her drink and was leaning forward beginning to collect the teacups. It was a cue for Father Peter to leave but he refused to take it. Something was not right.

'Sorry to hark back to that night, Maureen, but was that the last time you spoke to Jenny?'

'Yes,' she said firmly.

'You were going to go and see her, weren't you, Maureen?' Jack said.

'But I didn't.' Her tone was sharp.

'No.' Jack smiled. 'Only because you couldn't manage the

97

smog and mist. Perhaps if you had reached her you could have stopped the killer.'

Maureen was so still she seemed like a statue. Jack rambled on, 'She did set off but the traffic was too bad. It took her ages to get back.'

Father Peter said, 'It took me about three-quarters of an hour to reach the harbour from Saint Mary Mag's; the visibility was terrible.'

'Yes, Maureen got quite lost didn't you darling. She ended up in the supermarket. In a way, I'm glad she didn't get there. It's a bit callous of me but if she had, it might have been Maureen and not Jenny who was murdered. The thought gave me nightmares for weeks.'

'Well . . .' Maureen moved to collect the plates. Father Peter thanked them for their hospitality, offered to help with the washing up, and, for a change, hoped they would let him. But Maureen behaved as he normally wished all hosts would behave, and graciously refused.

A raw westerly wind was jiggling the daffodils planted in their neat front garden. Father Peter pulled up his collar and was glad of the warming effect of the whisky.

As he walked back in the direction of the church, he felt uneasy. Maureen was lying about something. Give me a child until he is seven, he thought, or until *she* is seven, and I will show you the man or woman. And the little child, Maureen, as skinny as a whippet before the age of seven, could never tell a lie without the most horrendous discomfort.

He remembered that the only time she had lied as a little girl was to cover up for another child in class, a boy who had broken a window. When the class was asked who had done it there had been a silence. Maureen's face had been crimson, and she had stared at her thumbnail, just as she had a few minutes ago.

And there was something else. What was it? He was aware of it when it happened and now he had forgotten. He sighed. What sort of arrogance did he possess? If the police could not solve the mystery, why should he think he was capable of doing so? But then again, he reasoned, he had prayed only to understand the anger, the reasons why the murders had happened.

Could she have been lying about Jenny? He knew in his heart that what she told him was the truth, that Jenny, like his own mother, was not the perfect person he'd wished her to be.

He pictured the three little girls in their school uniforms. Maureen had been the child who tried the hardest, the child who cried over the crucifixion, who wept with genuine repentance at confession, and tried so hard to live up to her catholicism. Stella had been the toughest little girl, very protective towards Maureen. She would take on bullies no matter how big or strong. She did not work as hard as Maureen did – it was not necessary. She was clever and robust. He remembered her beating the boys in the hundred-yard sprint, and down at the swimming baths, swimming like a little frog while urging Maureen on.

Jenny would make a great fuss about getting into the water, until the boys were in a frenzy, then streak across the pool with her beautifully shaped limbs. 'Give me a child until he is seven . . .' he murmured.

Jenny was always the most beautiful. She knew that all she had to do to get anything was to smile. She was bright but would work only at things that interested her. He remembered one of the primary school teachers telling him that she thought Jenny might be cheating in her homework. The woman suspected that either Maureen or Stella was letting Jenny copy her work.

It was as he was cleaning his teeth, just before going to bed, that he remembered what it was that had bothered him. Ever since he had known Maureen she had thanked God and the angels for good fortune, whether it was achieving one of the top ten places in class, or winning the egg-and-spoon race, which she once did. According to Jack, she had fulfilled a gambler's dream – won at roulette, a game of chance. Not once did she say, 'It was a miracle, Father,' or 'My guardian angel must have been watching over me,' as she usually did. No, he knew his girls: Maureen could tell a half truth or say nothing, but she could not blaspheme.

The promise of warm spring weather was broken on Friday, by the return of rain and sleet, and later by gales. The pain in his joints was excruciating. Monday arrived with a silent dawn, no prophetic screaming from the seagulls, just a gentle clucking from where they were perched on the chimney tops. There was a rise in the temperature, his aches and pains disappeared and he felt human again.

The bus dropped him at Sussex Square. He walked down towards the seafront, past the private gardens and terraces of four-storeyed houses with Ionic porches; then, after a short distance along the coast road, he came to the modern block of apartments where Stella lived.

When he reached the eighth floor and rang the bell he could smell the rich aroma of garlic and herbs in her cooking.

'You have inherited your father's talent as a chef,' he joked, when she opened the door.

She was wearing jeans and a bright yellow sweater. Her skin was tanned and she looked extremely fit but she was limping as she led him down the corridor and into the lounge.

'What's the matter with your leg?'

'I overdid it in Prague, trying to keep up with two young men, who I offered to show round the city. It took a very long soak in a hot bath to get rid of all the aches in my legs, I can tell you.'

She took his coat and pointed to his supermarket carrier bag. 'Is the Filofax in there?'

'Yes.'

For a moment she looked lost and undecided about what to do or say next. Then the jaw came forward, the teeth clenched and she said overbrightly, 'Oh good. I'll look at it after lunch.' She led him into the lounge. 'Would you like a glass of wine, Father?'

'That would be very welcome.'

'I've found a good warming red called Brunello. Just right for today, I thought.'

She was frowning as she poured his glass of wine. After she had seen that he approved of her choice, she returned to the kitchen. 'Lunch will be ready soon, Father,' she called.

He liked her lounge. It was L-shaped with views across the Marina and along the coast road. It was furnished simply and comfortably. Her furniture was covered in a coarse cream-coloured material, and daubed with orange cushions. The design was modern with straight clean lines. There was a glass-topped chrome dining table by the south-east-facing window on which lay bright orange place settings of a coarse weave. Apart from the bright spots of orange, the room was mainly decorated in a mixture of soft pale lemon and cream. Chrome and glass shelving held a set of the latest hi-fi equipment with a library of CDs and cassettes, books and magazines. There was no bric-a-brac. No room for clutter in her life. Tad's telescope stood by the balcony windows.

'Can I be of any help?' He wandered down the corridor where he could hear the clatter of plates in the kitchen.

'No, just relax Father, I'll be two minutes.'

What should have been a second bedroom was her study. He peered through the door. It was stark white and, except for some black metal shelving and bright orange filing cabinets, the walls were lined with books. Her semi-circular desk faced the window. On it was her word-processor, beside which lay a pile of neatly typed paper.

On a separate table by the door was her answerphone, telephone directories and address book. On the metal shelves were her tape recorder, binoculars, camera, and all her other journalist's equipment, mobile phone, portable radio and portable TV.

'Coming through,' she said.

He hurried back to the dining table and she entered with a large dish of penne covered in a wonderful meat sauce. He sat down at the table sipping his wine and savouring the anticipation of the lunch while she returned to the kitchen to fetch some warm french bread and a wooden bowl of tossed green salad.

'I really enjoyed the daytrip to Prague, Father. Two young men – they must have been in their early twenties, unemployed – they apparently write about twenty letters a week applying for jobs. Well, they'd saved up some money from their unemployment benefit, waited until two days before the flight, and, when the last few places were reduced to half the price, they bought their tickets. Their thrill at travelling to a city, normally way beyond their means, was wonderful. I've done the whole piece about showing them round the city, and their enthusiasm.

'It was sad, too. They were seeing well-dressed young people full of optimism, clean streets and beautiful buildings, when they knew their own, supposedly more affluent country had beggars in doorways, broken-down pavements and dirty streets, and certainly not a lot of optimism. They couldn't afford the lunch with the tour so I took them to a place I knew, up near Saint Vitus Cathedral. I told them how before the wall came down I had visited the cathedral and seen the priests trying to conduct a mass while tourists from Eastern Bloc countries wandered through, talking and walking right up to the altar.

'I told them I remembered crying and feeling so proud of those priests and the fact that I was part of the Catholic Church. It was lovely showing those lads around. I told them to study German and get themselves out of Britain. I think they will, too. But enough about my trip. What have you found out so far from the diary?'

Father Peter started at the beginning, with Bessie's reference to Sam. He told her about his discussions with Mike O'Reilly and how confused he was. She listened intently while making sure he helped himself to salad, then disappeared into the kitchen and returned with some Brie.

'I've put the coffee on. I'll just look through the Filofax while you have some cheese,' she said.

When she unwrapped the Filofax all the bright cheerfulness vanished. She held the book reverently while she fought a terrible moment of anguish. Then, jaws clenched, she began to skim the pages, fighting her sadness with sheer concentration. While he ate his cheese he watched her turning the pages. She looked just as she did as a child, he thought, wearing a slight frown, chewing the inside of her bottom lip. There was a determination to understand. She challenged whatever book it was to reveal its story. He had removed the photograph from the back wallet. He did not want to let Stella know Bessie's secret yet.

'How did the Filofax arrive Father? By post?'

'No, a soldier delivered it.'

'A soldier?'

'He'd just returned from Bosnia.'

'Are you sure it was a real soldier. I mean, could it have been someone pretending to be one. For example, could it have been an undercover policeman or someone like that?'

'No, I'm pretty sure he really was a young soldier.'

'You've talked to Mike – did he say whether anyone else

apart from Sam knew about Bessie's suspicions?' she said, looking at him intently.

'No, Bessie had made him promise not to say anything – he felt guilty telling me.'

'Good,' she said.

'Stella, can you understand why Bessie should be murdered over fishing quotas?'

'Not fishing quotas, Father, drugs. There was a large drug bust that autumn. Don't you remember? It was in all the national newspapers.'

'Drugs?' Father Peter said. 'What makes you so certain it was drugs? There was no mention of it in Bessie's diary.'

Stella went into the kitchen and returned with the coffee. When she spoke her expression was grim and she chose her words carefully.

'Bessie told me about Mike and Sam's worry about the fishing, and I got very concerned about what Bessie might be getting herself into. I suspected it might be drugs being smuggled in, and I knew that if she stumbled into that sort of organisation and screwed up, she could be in real danger.'

She stirred her coffee angrily. 'Father, even governments do deals with the cartels, and if you get in the way you've had it. I mean, all this rubbish and mealy-mouthed platitudes you get from world leaders about how they're going to stop "this terrible evil" is drivel. If there was a real political will to stamp out drugs, of *course* they could clean it up. Mao Tse Tung got rid of his problems with drugs in a week. He lined up all the pushers and shot them. But as long as you've got the various government agencies doing little deals with this and that group, keeping lines open in different countries to move arms, to appease some otherwise unfriendly country – the problem will never be solved. That's what makes the summary courts and the prosecution of some poor idiot growing some marijuana in a plant-pot so ridiculous, and

104

hypocritical. Sorry about that. I get so angry. Do you mind if I smoke?'

'I thought you'd given it up.'

'I did, but sometimes it's a fag or bust – I mean you won't cough or anything will you? I'll sit over here and open the window.' She collected her cigarettes from a cupboard down the hallway, and moved her coffee over to the other side of the room.

After a deep inhalation, she calmed down, peered at him through a haze of smoke, and said, 'I told Bessie to leave the whole thing alone. That if the fishing quotas were being broken they'd soon get caught. Especially if fishermen like Sam were shouting their mouths off. But she asked me if I would go with Sam and see if he was telling the truth. I said I would only go if she did not tell Sam who it was that was going with him, and if he could pick me up outside the Marina. Because, Father, I knew that if it was as I suspected, my own life could be in danger.'

Stella looked suddenly so vulnerable. She had tucked up her knees and was squeezing her arms together so that her hands were almost in a praying position – with the cigarette sticking out of her fingers. Father Peter felt a great wave of compassion for this little fighter.

'A few days later, Bessie came back, having told Sam that she was sending someone she trusted. And they agreed that the pick-up would be down by the groyne, on the beach where he kept his hut, at nine o'clock on the Wednesday night. The others were leaving the harbour by nine-thirty, he said.'

She took a drag at her cigarette and laughed ruefully. 'She told me to dress warmly. 'Never cast a clout till May is out,' she said – as if I was going on an outing. I was scared, Father, but I was more scared for Bessie if she continued pushing for information from anyone else.

'On the night, I put on my wellingtons, some dark jeans

105

and a black anorak and covered my hair with a dark balaclava. I hoped that, if I was seen on board, I might pass for another fisherman. I took a holdall with me. In it I had my camera and binoculars, and because it was cold, and I didn't know how long we'd be at sea, a flask of coffee and some sandwiches.

'I met Sam as arranged by the groyne and helped him shove off in the little dinghy to where he'd anchored his small fishing boat. He'd already had a few drinks and I was really regretting volunteering for the trip. He did most of the talking and I kept giving him coffee and sandwiches, hoping he wouldn't drink too much. We were following the others at a distance of about two hundred yards. About one hour after we started off, they all turned off their lights and continued for another hour in the dark. There was so much blackness, so much sea. And then I saw the large trawler where the smaller boats were pulling up alongside. The catch was being lowered down to each boat in a net.

'When we got closer, I wriggled down the companion ladder dragging my holdall with me and I was able to shoot off a roll of film through the small opening above when we were right alongside. I got the name of the trawler and a lot of faces that were on deck. One of them was American, the one obviously in charge. He was in his late fifties. I got a wonderful shot of him – no thanks to Sam, who kept blocking my view. I kept whispering to him to move his head and get out of the way. They were shouting down at him to get closer for the drop. They lowered it down, calling him a few names. And then the stupid fool shouts back at them, "I can't be expected to listen to everyone can I?" And I said, "For Christ's sake shut up and get out of here fast." I heard them shout, "Who's that with you Sam?" And then it filtered through even Sam's drink-sodden brain that he'd blown it, so he opened up the throttle and set off like the clappers.

106

'As soon as we were far enough away from the trawler I climbed up on deck, checked we weren't being followed and then looked at the netful of fish. They were large fish, about five to six pounds each, but they had sunken eyes and their fins were slack. I poked through the net at one and it felt cold, as if it had been frozen, but where I'd prodded the flesh it had left an indentation. I knew they weren't fresh or even recently caught. I took some pictures of them and then Sam shouted, "Do you want one for your supper?"

'The corners of the nets were tightly bound with wire, which made me even more sure about my suspicions. I managed to prise the end of the wire free and I took one of the fish and put it into my holdall. Then I tightened up the wire again and hoped for Sam's sake they weren't counting the fish.

'I asked Sam where he normally dropped the catch, and he said tonight they were supposed to be picked up in the Marina. I told him to drop me back first where he picked me up. I felt sure he wasn't going to get away with having had a stranger on board, and I didn't want to run into any trouble.

'And then he came over and inspected the fish. We'd had more coffee and he must have been more sober and aware than usual. "These are bloody funny fish," he said.

'When we got back, I ran like hell, taking the back-street route to my flat. I've never been so glad to get home. When I cut the fish open, there it was, a large packet of heroin stuffed inside. I put in on the table, on a background of white paper and photographed it. I developed the pictures myself.

'When I phoned Bessie the day after the trip and told her what I knew, she was appalled. I warned her not to say anything to either Sam or Mike, or indeed to anyone else. I told her I was developing the photographs and when they were ready I would post them to Lewes.

'Later, after Sam's body was found, I posted everything

from a post office in Haywards Heath. The pictures, the sealed-up fish and drugs, they were all sent to the drugs squad in Lewes. After Sam's death we waited to see if anything happened, and then as time went past we became more confident that we'd got away with it and that the drug squad were obviously checking things out.

'Then when the robbery happened we thought it might have been the drugs people. If only Bessie hadn't talked to that local reporter, those damned phone calls wouldn't have started, confusing us. We were so scared that it might be the drugs people after us. I kept telling Bessie not to say anything to anyone. But she must have talked to the wrong person. And that's why she was murdered.'

Large tears were rolling down her face. Father Peter felt close to tears himself.

'Shall I put some more coffee on, Father?' she said.

'Yes, I think that would be a good idea. I'll just use your bathroom, if I may.'

He rinsed his face and slowly washed his hands in a pleasantly perfumed soap. Her bathroom, like the rest of the flat, was simply decorated in a plain white with very little clutter. She didn't have most of the paraphernalia that most women seemed to have near the basin. Just some talcum powder, toothpaste, toothbrush and some dental cleaning tablets. He thought of her fighting her fear to help Bessie. Of her silence after Bessie's death. To have kept all this to herself. What courage the woman had. He remembered how thin and fragile she had been when she was brought back from her African jail. To have gone through all that and yet to have still volunteered to help Bessie was to have almost the dedication of a Jesuit, he thought.

As he was returning to the lounge, he heard the telephone ringing, then Stella's softly spoken response. He wandered over to the veranda windows and looked towards the Marina. He had not been back there since Jenny's death.

Unlike the gloomy place haunting his memory, the small stretch of land reclaimed from the sea looked bright and peaceful. He could see yachts in the dry dock being painted. Four fishing boats about half a mile out to sea were returning early, lining up and gauging the strength and position of the wind as they headed towards the harbour entrance.

'Father, I've got to go and meet the editor of the *Telegraph* tomorrow.'

He had been so lost in thought that he had not heard Stella's return. 'Is that a good thing for you?' he asked.

'Well, if all goes well, I'll be their Warsaw correspondent.'

'Warsaw?' He felt a great sense of loneliness, and as anxious as an old parent fearing the imminent departure of a child. Stella was so much a part of his life.

'How long will you be there?'

'About three years.'

'When will you have to leave?'

'Well, if I get it – oh, and I hope I do – I'll be leaving at the end of May.'

He realised how much he would miss her, his first baptised one. He might not ever see her again. There were hints that he was going to be put out to grass. When he saw the bishop recently the man had asked with concern about his aches and pains, and said, 'Perhaps, Peter, we can make sure that you spend next winter in Spain.'

He wanted to ask her about Jenny but didn't want to spoil her happier mood.

Instead he asked, 'When do you go off on your next project?'

'In a fortnight's time,' she replied. She grinned. 'I'm off to Florida. I can top up my tan on the cruise to the Bahamas, American style. Then I hang about in Miami for a while waiting to pick up a British ship at Fort Lauderdale to see how they look after you on the voyage to Bermuda. Then I stay with the ship until it docks in Southampton.'

'Could we talk again before you go?' he asked. 'Sure, I'll be here. Could I keep Bessie's diary for a little while?' Her face was wistful. He could not refuse her. But he still needed to know about Jenny.

'Stella, do you know who made those nuisance calls?'

She looked unhappy and was very reluctant to tell him.

'Yes, I do, Father.'

'I've already been told who it was,' he said. 'I just want it confirmed.' She was silent.

'I know who it was, Stella.'

'The person who made those calls was sick, and basically cruel, because she wanted power over the person on the other end of the phone. She called the wrong person and because she didn't realise what she had started she invited her own death. But she didn't deserve to be murdered.'

'I wouldn't have called Jenny cruel,' Father Peter said.

'Why, Father? Do you think she was any different from anyone else? We can all be cruel. Perhaps some of us express our cruelty without making stupid telephone calls. But we are all capable of cruelty. There were many things I liked about Jenny. She was generous, although sometimes it was more like a trading of favours. But I loved her as a friend and I admired the fact that she could have cut herself off from her roots and just mixed with the very rich, but wanted more. I wish she'd gone to college instead of that posh finishing school. I think she always resented the fact that Maureen and I had been to university.

'She only wanted to be a JP because Maureen was one. Not because she had any feelings for justice. Why should she? Life had dealt her the most fortunate hand – she knew nothing of injustice. She had never had to fight for anything. Although,' she started to laugh, 'she did try to understand, theoretically anyway.'

She laughed again. 'I remember her very earnestly trying to tell some woman up before the bench for not paying her TV licence how she could pay off a fine at the rate of one pound a week if she cut back on food and heating. Jenny hadn't a clue what food cost, or heating, and the blouse she was wearing was worth more than a month's social security payments, which was all the defendant had to live on.'

She became solemn again. 'I think, Father, that she must have plagued the wrong person with those calls. I also think that, because she took Bessie to Sam's funeral, it was wrongly presumed that Jenny was the person in the boat with Sam. That's why I think she was murdered.'

They sat in silence, both locked into their own thoughts.

'Did the police know Jenny made those calls?' Father Peter asked.

'They might have suspected,' she replied. 'But I was useless at dialling at the right time – and they had to catch her calling three times for a prosecution. I think when Bessie told the other magistrates to report the calls, Jenny became more careful when she made them. But I think they must have known it was her.'

He told her about what he'd heard about the shooting and she sighed and began to rub her temples.

'Stella, do you think if Charles found out about his trawlers being used for drugs the people behind it all could have killed him?'

She gave another long sigh.

'Do you think I should hand the Filofax over to the police in case it would help?' he said.

'What would it achieve, Father? It won't bring them back. It will just stir everything up again. Their families would be bothered by journalists. Remember what it was like. I mean what is your real need Father?'

'I suppose I just want to understand the anger that leads to murder,' he said.

'And I want to understand how the establishment of a country can murder society,' she replied. 'I didn't resign from the bench because I was scared, Father: I left because I had absolutely no respect for the system. There was no such thing as justice. My faith decreed that there was a higher justice from which no one escapes, but I could no longer serve a Crown that flouted its own laws, and that held its people in such contempt.'

'I suppose I want to know why Charles was killed because I knew him too,' he said simply.

Her telephone began to ring again and he decided it was time to leave. He felt a great sadness. He had seen Stella's anger, he knew his own and Maureen's. He had listened to Bessie's anger about injustice. It was a collective madness hurting people's minds. What was that quote from Euripides? 'Whom God wishes to destroy, he first makes mad.' Was Britain in a state of rage? If so, where would this anger take the country?

She was still on the telephone when he waved from the door.

'I'll ring you Father,' she whispered.

He wandered down towards the Marina. The sunlight was harsh and seemed to pinch at his skin. Past the supermarket and the large public house, there was a café. There were some tables outside and an old lady sat wrapped in knitted shawls sipping coffee. Father Peter took the table nearby and ordered tea. They were like some painting, he and the old woman, sitting still in the sun, he thought. The painting would be called *Despondent Age*, he mused.

A tall man walked into the café area and sat on the far-side table. Father Peter guessed his age to be about forty. He was attractive with an unusual mole on his cheek. The mole was almost a large beauty spot, of the type for which the old film star Margaret Lockwood was famous. Father Peter wondered whether he was unemployed like so many of the young men walking Brighton's streets. The man sat reading a paper and when Father Peter's tray of tea arrived he ordered a coffee.

The teapot was made of the type of metal that dangerously conducted the heat. Father Peter wrapped his handkerchief round the handle with a good deal of irritation, and tried not to spill the rather weak tea into his saucer. Was it his imagination or was the young man with the mole amused by his antics.

Having managed to pour the tea successfully, he sat thinking about what he now knew.

Sam, with other fishermen, had been carrying fish containing drugs to collection points in Brighton. Sam had misunderstood the seriousness of his position and had involved Bessie, Mike and Stella. Whoever murdered Sam had known or guessed that there was a woman on board Sam's boat that night. When Bessie and Jenny turned up at Sam's funeral, *someone* must have seen them. The men at the funeral that Bessie had written about must have given the murderer the information. Or possibly one of the men had been the murderer. After Sam's death, Stella had posted the photographs to the drug squad. Perhaps the murderer knew this.

If Bessie knew the murderer and had talked to him, he had probably killed her. If Jenny had been telephoning him and he suspected she knew about the drugs, that was why she was killed.

He sipped his tea thoughtfully. He must have been the last one Jenny spoke to when she asked him to come so she could make her confession. And she was full of remorse when she called. Perhaps she realised how cruel, as Stella called it, she'd been. Whoever killed her must have known she was there.

If she called him first, there was a good chance that it

was Charles who killed her. Then it was possible that it was Charles who murdered Bessie. She knew him – she might have challenged him despite Stella's warnings. But who robbed Jenny's safe? Charles didn't need the money. Perhaps he thought she had the packet of heroin missing from the load of fish. That was possible. After killing Jenny something must have gone wrong, which was why *he* was killed.

Father Peter sipped his tea, remembering his last night's dream. It had been a strange dream. He had found himself in the shadow of a hill. All he could see was dark, damp grass. He had started climbing and it had been terribly steep. When he was near the top, he had heard groaning and seen two hands protruding from some wood. As he reached the summit, he found himself in the shadow of the cross, and able to see the poor weary head crowned in thorns. He had wanted to lift Him off, help Him, pull out the nails. He had approached from behind, placing his arms around His knees, and had tried to support the weight. But the pain had been agonising. He had woken with a terrible sense of anguish, in such a depth of sadness that he had failed to share His terrible burden.

And Stella had borne that burden of failure, the failure to help Bessie and Jenny. She had borne it all alone.

After he'd paid his bill and was about to leave the café and attempt the walk home along the seafront, he noticed the younger man get up and approach the waiter. Then, lost in thought, Father Peter started walking towards the Palace Pier. He went through all the facts. He knew them by heart. Was he overlooking something?

Away from the shelter of the Marina he became exposed to the cold, south-westerly wind. He pulled his scarf on tight and tried to see through watering eyes.

What was the most common confession that he heard each week? he asked himself. The answer was always sex of some kind or other. What if Jenny's murder had nothing whatsoever to do with Sam and his fish but was a lovers' tiff? The commonest motive for murder was passion. But who shot Charles? Jenny's husband? Why not? He stopped between the piers and leaned against the promenade railings, staring out to sea. Was there one murderer or two? The Boss knew. He smiled to himself. If and when He wanted him to know the truth, the Boss would show him.

He lifted his head and looked up at the seagulls flying in air corridors over the roofs of the hotels. Another man was leaning against the railings. Unless his eyes were deceiving him it was the man from the café. Father Peter continued walking. The pale yolk of a sun was beginning its descent, moving through smeared white strands of cloud. It was getting much colder and the sudden gusts of wind were making his ears ache.

Just as he was passing the Grand Hotel, he saw the green light. He stopped in amazement. Old Sam and Mike were right. It was definitely green. From the end of the rotting West Pier a cloud of starlings rose into the sky and began to swoop into patterns and shapes. As they soared upwards, their wings catching the light, the flock of birds became a thin line against the green-blue sky. Then they turned, becoming a collective energy of intention. Slowly they began to swoop, forming a figure eight. As they reached the end of the second loop, they turned, becoming one with the sky, before changing into a cloud moving inland away from the sea. Like the starlings, Father Peter left the seafront and walked uphill through the town towards the church. The gales reached Brighton two hours later.

6

She was falling through an eternal tunnel of infinite grief,
the walls echoing with the sounds of her own anguished
sobbing. Regret and guilt pulled her again to the blinking
light of the answerphone, where the tinny voice screamed
that there were two messages, both from Jenny – the second
message being the last words spoken before her death.

Stella was suffocating with fear. She wanted to telephone
back, to tell Jenny to be careful, to escape before she was
killed, but the doorbell was ringing and her arms and legs
were paralysed by terror. Maureen's voice was pleading with
her, 'Please Stella, open the door, let me in.' She turned the
handle slowly, then Maureen seized her hands, squeezing
them in desperation.

'Oh God Stella, what have I done? What am I going to
do? You've got to help me.'

Stella was trying to make sense of murder and madness,
and Maureen was pulling at her shoulders.

'Would you like a hot towel?'

Sweating with panic, she scrambled out from under the
blanket only to be confronted by the calm efficient face of
the air hostess. Gratefully, she took the hot, cologne-soaked
towel and pressed it to her eyes.

The hauntings went on, forever waiting in dark corners,
a parade of future visions of purgatory for her guilt-ridden
soul. All the things she had not done, left undone through

fear. All the things she had done with the insane confidence of anger.

Blinds were being pushed back to reveal a hot afternoon sun. There was an hour before landing at Miami airport. It would be taken up with afternoon tea and form-filling.

Her legs had not swollen. The travel firm were determined to woo her favour so they had paid for her to travel Club Class. The comfort of it was overwhelming. It was a long time since she had managed to sleep on a plane. There was so much more room than in World Traveller where the seats seemed to be designed for anorexic midgets with giraffe necks.

She decided to get to the lavatory before a queue formed. Clutching her holdall and complimentary bag of refreshing goodies, eye balm, rosewater spray, flannel, toothpaste and toothbrush, she hurried up the aisle.

Her T-shirt was wet with the perspiration from her nightmare. Once inside the cubicle, she stripped off and stood naked, allowing her skin to throw off the clamminess of stress. After she had rinsed her face and cleaned her teeth, gargling with the contents of a small bottle of mouthwash, also in the complimentary bag, then sponged her entire body with the flannel, she felt calmer. She looked at her face. Apart from the slight puffiness caused by the changes in altitude, she looked remarkably fresh and alert, but the dream lingered in her mind.

When she'd last spoken to Maureen she had begged her to make her confession, so that, when she returned from cruising, she could take her last communion with Father Peter, before leaving for Warsaw. She wanted the old priest to know everything – and to understand. She wondered whether Maureen would go to confession. She should – Maureen was looking worn with guilt; it was really making her ill.

Stella gave a long drawn-out sigh. The situation was so

118

complex. She could not make her confession until Maureen had been. Their confessions were so interlinked that she would implicate Maureen in her own. Stella now regretted having agreed to report on the cruising experience.

It was the wrong moment to be away from Brighton. There was so much to arrange before leaving for Warsaw, and she would like to have spent more time talking with Maureen, to give her the reassurance she needed. But she had to honour her commitment to the women's magazine. The article was well paid, and it was not their fault that the correspondent's job came up afterwards. Also, she wanted to keep all her options open for the future, and that included the goodwill of travel feature-editors. The Warsaw job might not work out. At least by honouring her commitments, there was always the chance, if anything went wrong, that she could take up travel reporting again.

Despite the drying effects of the air-conditioning, a tear began to form in the corner of her right eye. She could see Father Peter's face, clean and wholesome, a gentle, refulgent expression of faith. How desperately she wanted to join in, to be part of that constancy again, and how she feared weeping like some emotional religeuse, watched with pity by some anonymous onlooker, sanctified by a clear conscience. At each mass she sat in an abstraction of religious appreciation, listening to the kyrie with a critic's ear, and she always left the church with an aching regret that, as with other moments in her past, she had chosen to be safe and insignificant, because of fear. She loved Father Peter, knew it would be his last Easter at Saint Mary Magdalene's before he left for Spain, and she wanted him to understand.

She splashed herself with some cologne and put on some clean clothes she had packed in her holdall. It would be four in the afternoon when they arrived, and eighty degrees Fahrenheit, a vast improvement on the cold wet weather she had left behind. She would send a card to Maureen as soon as she reached the hotel. She always sent her a postcard and bought her a duty-free present whenever she went on a trip. They were bound together by their early years, by the memory of sharing the same staircase, the same address, the pavement where they played hopscotch, outside their shabby flats. They had depended on each other to get to school. Look left, look right and left again, before crossing the street. And Jenny would be waiting outside her house, ready to join them, with some exotic story to tell.

Stella and Maureen had shared their rebellions in the convent, planned their futures during the holidays from university. They had cheered each other on, each proud of the other's achievements, wept for each other's great hurts. Maureen had cried uncontrollably when Stella told her about her experiences in the African jail, and Stella had tried to comfort her when she found a distraught Maureen in the court lavatory, weeping while trying to form a judgement on a shoplifter ground down by poverty. Stella knew she had once paid a fine for an old woman unable to pay her television licence fee.

'Bessie's right, Stella,' Maureen had said. 'Only those who truly understand poverty should judge the thief.' To which she had argued, 'And do you think that only those who understand the consuming nature of anger should judge the murderer?'

'Do you think there is such a person who can understand all these human passions? I don't think even Solomon could cope with some of the problems we face in court,' Maureen replied.

They had argued the philosophy of justice continually, raging about various judges' stupid decisions, until finally they had decided that man was incapable of administrating true justice, and that only God in His infinite wisdom could judge anyone.

She was met at the airport by an efficient woman travel

agent, carrying a clipboard with Stella's name displayed. She was called Wendy, and wore the harassed look of the overworked and a short skirt that hardly complimented her spindly black-stockinged legs. Stella's luggage was 'organised' quickly and she was escorted with rapid speed to a chauffeur-driven white stretch limousine.

They were really going right over the top, she thought, but it was a novel experience to be treated like a film star. She could not live up to all the grandeur. She was not dressed for the occasion. She sat at the back of the limo, dressed in her jeans and yellow padded bomber-jacket, alone – Wendy was going ahead in her own car – and felt quite absurd as she gazed down the leather-seated tube.

As they drove from the airport, she noticed the amount of work and investment in the streets. Buildings were all painted, or in the process of being restored and repaired.

'You should'a seen it after the hurricane,' the chauffeur told her. But, they had repaired and invested back into their own city, she thought, comparing Miami with poor old Brighton, where the government had not even declared a state of emergency when the town was hit by the hurricane of 1987. There was no optimistic investment there. Just an endless patching up of roads or piecemeal pavement repairs, all because of the lack of money.

Why, she wondered, couldn't the money men invest in the British towns – paint the buildings, invest in their own people? They were quick enough to invest abroad. One restored theatre or civic building was a cause for celebration. Someone usually ended up with a commendation for the effort. It was not expected by the public any more that buildings should automatically be looked after, or kept clean, the sign of any mature civilisation. She had once heard some American tourists say, 'We didn't realise Brighton had been so badly bombed in the war,' and felt a deep anger and shame. The blitzed look in the town had nothing to do with the war. It was just a series of speculative building programmes that had never materialised when the companies beginning the projects went bankrupt.

Wendy arrived at the Airport Hilton first, greeted Stella profusely again when she arrived, then sat her in a plush armchair in the foyer while she sorted out the room. She was then escorted to the twelfth floor in a smooth, silent lift and led into a suite.

They were determined that she should enjoy this working holiday, she thought. To give the Americans their due, they really knew how to look after someone when they wanted the favour of a good write-up, and she was very happy about the bribery.

After arranging to collect her the following afternoon to escort her to the docks, Wendy departed, leaving Stella to enjoy the luxury of her suite.

Both sides of the lounge had large windows. On one side she overlooked the airport's runway. A steady queue of planes taxied along the flight strip where they paused before taking off. Small executive jets followed the larger international planes, departing at intervals of about ninety seconds. Between the airstrip and the hotel was a main road on which flowed a continuous stream of traffic. The soundproofing, plus the steady sound of the air-conditioning, ensured a minimal noise level. The other window overlooked palm trees, a turquoise swimming pool and exotic gardens.

The furniture was all made of walnut and designed in the Art Deco style. There was a large sofa and comfortable easy chairs, a desk with a telephone-fax machine, a cabinet with stereo equipment, a drinks sideboard, and by the windows a circular dining-table on which stood a large arrangement of silk flowers.

Stella sat at the table and gazed at the panoramic view. It

was pink, she decided. Miami gave the impression of having a pinkish hue.

She explored the bathroom. Everything was spotless. Towels were white and fluffy, and there was a large selection of soaps, shampoos and lotions.

The bedroom window overlooked the gardens. The strong sunlight was subdued by soft billowing net curtains. The double bed looked smooth and inviting. Stella flopped on to it and slept soundly for three hours.

She woke refreshed and hungry, and wandered into the lounge to watch Miami at night. A steady line of headlights moved continuously along the road by the airport. Airborne planes, their lights flashing, headed for distant cities. She found the lamp switches, sat at the desk and planned her evening. She would have a luxurious bath, go down to the restaurant and have a real American steak. Then she would start on her feature. She also wanted to see some American television news.

She dressed in one of her designer-supplied outfits – a cream silk dress with a soft taupe coloured waistcoat – and was glad her legs were still tanned from her time in the Caribbean. She felt clean, pampered and expensive. She headed for the bar.

America was the home of the bar pianist, she mused, listening to the soft, gentle tones, while she sipped a cocktail that resembled a fruit salad. The pianist began to play, *The Birth of the Blues*, and Stella remembered being with Colin in the Blue Note Bar down in Greenwich Village in the early eighties, just before she left for the fateful trip to South Africa. She remembered Colin teaching the barman how the British drank whisky – the poor fellow could not cope with the fact that Colin did not want ice with his drink, just water. Confused, he had returned with the glass filled to the brim. Colin had said, 'Perhaps they think we're a bit mimsy asking for water – don't they always drink it neat?

Don't they always say, "Hit me again" like the cowboys or Humphrey Bogart?'

They had taught the barman to bring a jug. He had really appreciated the lesson. 'Well I've really learnt something tonight,' he'd said. Stella wondered whether the barman now offered the odd tourist ordering whisky a choice: 'the American or British way?'

The people sitting at tables near her were speaking mostly Spanish. There were a few Japanese but English was being spoken by very few people. It was almost like being in Southern Europe, she thought. She decided that she would be able to manage a New-York-style steak tonight. She never ate beef in England. She usually substituted minced chicken or New Zealand lamb to accompany her pastas ever since the beef scare. But here she felt bold enough to go for meat. She felt positively carnivorous.

The Colombian waiter found her a quiet table. She had started with garlic-laden mushrooms, and was halfway through her mammoth, New York steak and Caesar salad, when she saw him enter the dining-room. At first she thought it was a trick of the imagination. It couldn't possibly be him, she thought. But if by chance it was, what was he doing in Miami? She picked up her glass of wine and placed it in front of her eyes, momentarily believing, like a monkey, that if her eyes were covered she would be invisible to predators. She peeped with one eye round the side of the glass. It was definitely him. She picked up her key and tucked it quickly inside her handbag. She wondered whether he knew she was here. Was it possible he had followed her? What on earth was John Smith doing here?

Suddenly, she felt apprehensive. She saw him look round the room and then he spotted her. She heard him speak to the waiter in Spanish, and then she watched him make his way over to her table.

'Would you prefer to be alone, or may I join you?'

'Help yourself,' she replied ungraciously. She felt the beginnings of indigestion.

'Is the steak good?'

'They serve very large portions when it's a New York steak – but it is very good.' She wiped her mouth with the napkin. 'So, what brings you to Miami? Don't tell me it's a police convention.'

'No, I'm on holiday, but I can't afford to keep up with journalists in Club Class and suites – I have to travel World Traveller and stay in cheaper accommodation. But I'm on the cruise – in a cheaper cabin, I'm afraid. But at least you'll have your own private detective.' He grinned at her.

'John Smith, you're mad,' she laughed.

'I confess I had clocked up some air miles when I was sent off on duty travels. You are looking quite beautiful, if you don't mind me saying so.'

She found herself blushing with pleasure and panicking at the same time. Either he was absolutely bonkers and fancied her wildly – there were men who followed women to the ends of the earth but she had never seen herself as a recipient of such ardour – or he was playing a clever game because he suspected she knew something. And, if he thought that, she had better keep her brain clear, and stay cool. It was difficult because he was being charming and witty, and she did find him very handsome. Or was it the element of danger that attracted her?

He managed to eat nine-tenths of his steak while she was beaten after three-quarters.

He told her he was in a hotel in the Art Deco district in Miami Beach. He wanted time to explore it before the boat left. His face was almost boyish with enthusiasm. She wondered whether his apparent innocence helped to make him a good detective, then felt guilty for such cynicism.

After two cappuccinos, they lapsed into silence. She wondered whether he was expecting her to ask him to her suite. If so he was going to be disappointed. He surprised her by saying, 'Well, the trip has caught up with me, I'm afraid. I'm bushed. I'd better drive back. It's about half an hour from here.'

'I'll see you aboard,' she replied.

He took her hand and kissed her fingertips, then got up from the table.

'Goodnight, Stella,' he said.

'Goodnight,' she mumbled.

She decided to wait for a while before leaving. She ordered another coffee and suddenly craved a cigarette. The kiss had undermined all her common sense. Her arm was tingling with pleasure, and a part of her wanted to run after him and shout, 'Let's not waste time – come up and share my wonderful suite.'

She ordered some cigarettes from the waiter and pulled her notebook and biro out of her bag. Work, she told herself. That is why you're here, to complete a travel feature. She began writing, fighting her confused emotions with the application of her mind to words.

Later, wrapped in her towelling dressing-gown, she gazed from her lounge windows. There were fewer flights leaving the airport now but the steady rhythm of traffic continued. Was it really possible, she wondered, that a policeman was romantic enough to be willing to travel this far to see her? Was he really in the Art Deco district or was he prowling around the hotel? She went to the suite door and locked it securely. Or was John Smith here for some other reason?

She found a plate of strawberries dipped in chocolate in the centre of the lounge table with a card saying, COMPLIMENTS OF THE MANAGEMENT. She felt wide awake and slightly mad. Clutching the plate of strawberries, she sat on the sofa and turned on the television.

She switched from channel to channel in a vain attempt to find some decent news coverage. Reporters seemed more concerned about their appearances than the content of their stories. The women had that stiff fixed smile of those who have resorted to plastic surgery, while the men seemed either to have hair that had been badly dyed, so that it did not match their skin pigment, or to be wearing ill-fitting toupees that did not quite cover their own hair.

News programmes were made up of jokes, tag-lines and smiles. Entertainment with a capital E rather than journalism. The same thing was beginning to creep into British television. The night-time British news coverage was now more a form of tabloid news, a comforting fluffy story at the end of each harrowing disaster. 'Leave them with a smile' seemed to be the philosophy of the editors, but don't, what ever you do, let them *think* too much or give them too much information.

One of the American channels was devoted to the O. J. Simpson murder trial. Defence lawyers postured, glancing towards the cameras like bad actors. The camera lens zoomed in to reveal every pause or thought on a witness's face.

How could a country with something as brilliant as the Declaration of Independence trivialise and insult the law? she wondered. How could a country that would spend so much on its cities pollute its nation's mind with pulp? Was this the road down which Britain was following? If so, she was glad she was leaving for Warsaw. Perhaps the influence of Eastern Europe would halt the trivialising effects of American culture on Western Europe, Britain in particular.

She switched to another channel. A presenter was discussing a trial, asking a defendant whether he wanted to say sorry for what he had done. The alleged offender's lawyer was advising him not to reply to this or that question. 'What the hell is he doing on TV?' Stella yelled at the television. 'The case is sub judice for goodness' sake.'

She turned off the set in disgust and returned to watch the planes on the airport runway. Bessie had warned so many times about the authority of law being eroded by bureaucratic compromise. 'If people don't feel they are getting real justice,' she had announced to the retiring-room full of magistrates, 'they will resort to taking the law into their own hands, both at national and international levels.'

How long would it be, Stella wondered, before the people here became sick of popularity politics, facile sentimentality and show business, and politically correct justice. Britain and America were both powder kegs of disillusionment, waiting for the spark of cultural revolution, while wisdom remained unseen, silent among the ravings of madness on the airwaves. Wisdom was the gentlest voice, without fear or favour, full of love and ignored by those pursuing the trivial.

She watched the headlights of planes in the distance, circling the airport, ready to land. There were those who wanted higher intelligences from outer space, or Mother Nature, to judge the irresponsibility of man. These people craved wise judgement, free of the manipulative organisations, the power-seekers, the money interests and the self-indulgent extroverts. Like herself, she thought sadly, they were unable to hear the wise answers from prayer.

Beyond the calm waters of Miami harbour, in the Straits of Florida, the sea was much rougher. Stella passed John Smith on the way to her allotted lifeboat station, during the compulsory emergency drill. He helped her to tie her lifebelt properly, and then, seeing she was carrying her tape recorder and was obviously working on the feature, arranged to join her for dinner at the second sitting.

Her brief from the women's magazine editor was to compare the different styles of cruising offered by the British and Americans. Cruising was going to be the holiday travel of the future. They were even building a golf course on one ship to appeal to the golfers.

It was easy to see why people wanted to cruise. Travel was smoother than all the hassle of flying, booking into an unknown hotel and searching for places to eat or for entertainment. Everything was arranged for you; even the exploration of another country was planned, giving the traveller the security of being surrounded by fellow countrymen on a conducted tour. The Americans wanted the comfort and lifestyle they knew and understood, unlike the more individualist Europeans.

'Watch my lips' made absolute sense as greetings of 'and how are you today?' and 'you're welcome' were uttered by the corporation-trained staff. They were totally confused by a simple request, or complaint, that did not fit in with their carefully tailored formula. Blank-eyed responses confirmed for Stella that no one listened, but everyone performed – so the need for 'watch my lips' had obviously been a cry from a president's heart for a nation's attention.

Every steward wanted to tell a story, everyone in a uniform wanted to be a star. All American society, it seemed, were actors on the boards of the American Dream theatre, but they had been given words they did not understand, and had been handed only that part of the script that the producers deemed necessary for the continued commercial success of the play.

Never had Stella felt so European as when she sat down at the second sitting for dinner on the cruise ship. The sound of American voices engulfed her, while Portuguese, Polish and British waiters sympathetically hovered, using the words, 'you're welcome,' and 'enjoy,' before being hauled off at the end of the meal to sing *America the Land of the Free*. Everything was, 'It's Showtime.'

The attempt to turn immigrant workers into have-a-nice-day automotons was not working. These were people intelligent and aggressive enough to have escaped their own countries for the chance to earn big bucks – they were predators, not compliant, easygoing creatures brought up from the early years with the American dream. Their lips curled as they said, 'Have a nice day.' There was a glint in the eye as they mumbled, 'You're welcome.'

'I'm here for the money, love,' said one cockney lad, when she asked him why he was working on an American ship. 'It's better than the dole.'

She was glad of John's company. They heard one woman on the table talking to her husband about their sullen daughter, sitting next to them, who had not wanted to come on the trip. Stella saw the twinkle in John's eye when they both overheard the woman say, 'I could really twist her into a pretzel.' She realised how long it had been since she was able to share a look with someone, or feel the comfort of knowing she was not alone in seeing the humour of a situation. It was all very well being an observer, a detached eye, but she was alone so often. Although Stella did not mind her own company, and enjoyed her work, it was the sharing again that made her realise how much she had missed having a man in her life.

John Smith did not intrude upon her space. When she was working, he would discreetly withdraw from any need for her attention.

'Did you ever take ballroom dancing lessons?' she asked him as she sipped her coffee. 'You seem to have a natural instinct for the right moves not to tread on someone's toes.'

'I was made to learn so I could partner my sisters at weddings, if no one asked them to dance.'

'Where were you brought up?'

'Gibraltar. My mother was Spanish and my father English.' He leaned back in his seat. 'Dancing also came in handy when I had to join a golf club. I was on a fraud case. At the golf club dance, I got a lot of information I needed when one lady was slightly tipsy during a waltz.'

'Is flirting part of your police training?' she asked.

'No, that's specialist knowledge you volunteer on your CV.' He shook his head. 'I thought I was bad, but you really are the most suspicious woman.'

'A cautious woman.'

'A female Freemason?'

'Oh, really!'

'Was there much of it on the bench when you were a magistrate?'

'Freemasonry?'

'Yes.'

'Well, I know everyone goes on about it, but I found all the masons to be very open about their membership. Occasionally, some defendant would scratch his ear or something, but I always found that the Freemasons would let the other two non-mason JPs decide the case, without any favouritism at all. It's no different from a Catholic coming up before a Catholic. Just because a mugger crosses himself doesn't mean those magistrates of the faith are going to let him off. Why, are you one? There are a lot of police who are Freemasons aren't there?'

'Yes there are, and no I'm not. Charles Nightingale was one, wasn't he?'

Alarm bells went off in her head. 'I think he was,' she replied.

'How did you get on with him?'

'I didn't know him very well.'

While they were watching a lavishly dressed floor show, the glasses on the table began to slide. The dancers were beginning to find it difficult to keep their balance, and the compere warned that they were running into a weather front. They were expecting winds of thirty knots, he said. A comedian

131

made light of it by leaning against the proscenium arch and delivering his jokes, which seemed mainly concerned with the problems people had with the family bathroom. Stella began to feel queasy.

John suggested going out on deck to get some fresh air. 'It's always best to go with the movement of the ship when it's rough,' he said.

She did feel better as soon as she left the air-conditioned atmosphere and stepped outside.

They started to walk towards the prow of the ship. Gusts of wind whipped her hair across her eyes. Holding it back from her face, she looked starboard across the blackness of the sea. About a mile away, moving parallel to their ship, Stella could see the brightly lit outline of another cruise-liner. It looked so vulnerable heaving up and down in the waves. The saying 'ships that pass in the night' took on a new meaning when she considered how insignificant they were, compared with the vast, dark and threatening ocean. They strode on until, just as they were approaching the curve of the bow, the force of the wind momentarily made her lose her balance. She fell towards the rail. John's hand grabbed her arm with a vicelike grip.

'I don't want to ruin this jacket by having to jump in to save you,' he yelled. 'Stop being so bloody independent and hold on to my arm.'

They walked on until they were able to lean against some strong ironwork in line with the prow of the ship. John put his arm round her shoulders and hugged her close to him. 'Now we'll ride the waves and you'll lose your seasickness,' he said.

It was exciting, watching the ship cut through the heaving, swirling movements of the waves. The sea spray lifted and fell across the decks, fine and dazzling in the lights. She tasted the salt moisture as it drifted over them.

When he kissed her she was unsure whether it was the

movement of the boat or the overwhelming passion that made her quite pleasurably giddy. Her observer self retreated and she was left in a sea of erotic emotions, enjoying the experience of shipboard romance. Inside his jacket she could feel the warm outline of his lean, strong body, his back muscles flexing under his crisp shirt. The observer self returned, tapping her consciousness with a reminder of work. She tried to shut it out, to pursue the state of abandonment, but it continued niggling away at her with fears of propriety, professionalism and the whole practicality of cabin complications. Reluctantly she withdrew from his passionate embrace.

'I've got to breathe for a while,' she shouted.

They watched the waves. The other cruise ship had pulled ahead and was leading the way.

He escorted her back to her cabin. She tried to hide her feelings of indecision. He helped her by saying, 'I'll see you at breakfast.' His lips were gentle. She closed the cabin door in a state of frustration and regret.

They disembarked at Nassau to the sounds of a steel band playing Calypso music. Teams of women tried to talk Stella into having her hair beaded, promising that the men in her life would really be turned on if her head was laden with strands of beads.

'Nothing would turn me off more than being hit in the mouth by beads,' John assured her.

Before leaving the ship they had been told of all the bargains waiting for them ashore. American matrons dragged their husbands towards John Bull's Emporium to buy expensive leather bags and perfume. The whole main street was geared up to sell to the tourist.

They took a pony and trap and set off to explore the island. They saw old streets of small, run-down, wooden colonial houses. Some were boarded up, others were mere shells of peeling paint. More affluent areas had beautifully maintained gardens and well-cared-for newer houses. But most of the investment was in the newly built banks and in the governor's house.

'So that's where our taxes go,' Stella said sourly, 'maintaining the governor's vast palatial premises. What do you think he does for all that expenditure?'

'Helps to look after the Queen's offshore accounts perhaps?' John suggested. Stella laughed.

'This place reminds me of Gibraltar,' John said. 'They've let that island fall into decay as well. Another place for duty-free goods and not much else. I hope the Spanish take it over. At least they'll get some decent pavements and some style rather than becoming like some run-down British seaside resort.'

'Do you feel more Spanish or English?' she asked him.

'I fluctuate between the two. But I think I'm detached about Britain. A full-blooded Englishman is a bit in awe of his traditions. I'm not. And you? How do you feel?'

'I'm like you, I think: detached. I've spent so much time abroad. I know a lot of colonials who have returned to England, and a lot of people like me, second-generation immigrants. They all feel more British than the British. I shall know how I feel about my Polish roots when I get to Warsaw.'

'When are you going there?'

'The end of May.'

'For how long?'

'About three years.'

'Three years.' He sounded shocked.

'I've just landed a correspondent's job. Three years tax free, all expenses paid.'

He was silent.

They passed by a market with stalls piled with fruit, vegetables, flowers and bright materials. Then she heard him say, 'I shall have to move quickly, won't I?'

134

It had been arranged for her to travel out to Coral Island, where gaudy parrots shrieked from the tops of trees as she headed towards the shark tanks and the stingray pools and then descended to the bottom of the sea bed through an underwater observatory. John came with her. After deciding he liked the saucer-eyed porgy – a blue fish with yellow scales – he disappeared while she made her notes. She found him waiting by the harbour.

'A present,' he said.

'What is it, an oyster?'

'Not just an oyster. It is an oyster guaranteed to have a pearl inside.' He undid the shell with a pocket knife and fished out a tiny white pearl.

'Thank you,'

'That's for sending me those wonderful pictures, and the fish stuffed with heroin, so we could tie up the drugs case.' Stella tried to conceal the fact that all saliva seemed to have drained from her mouth. Her smile felt smeared against her teeth.

He just would not give up, she thought. A policeman through and through. Never off duty. Waiting for her to let down her defences. She ran her tongue over her lips and forced a laugh.

'You mean the big drug bust that won you your promotion?'

His face was almost boyish with the sense of expecta-tion.

'That's right. We managed to get the American – the big man himself. Even Interpol hadn't managed to get him.'

'I seem to remember reading about it,' she said sweetly, 'but you have nothing to thank me for. But I'm grateful for the pearl. I'll use it in the feature.'

The tender taking them back to Nassau was having difficulty with more rough weather. Stella kept a tight hold on her camera and tape recorder, fearful that if she eased her grip she could lose them overboard. John sat opposite her and was watching her closely.

'I'm sorry you can't trust me, Stella,' he said. 'Surely to God you know that I know you sent them. I had two men undercover among the fishermen. It had been a long-term set-up, trying to get the big boys. You managed to get the photos our chaps couldn't get without arousing suspicion. The pictures helped to give us the proof we needed much earlier than we expected.'

She said nothing.

'Dear God, Stella,' he said exasperated by her taciturnity. 'OK. I couldn't prove you were the one who went out on the boat with the old fisherman.' Stella remained silent. The wind was causing her eyes to water. 'It's just a hunch, Stella,' John said. 'I trust most of my hunches, and I know I'm right about you. I'm sorry you can't trust me.'

She watched the harbour grow closer as the tender fought the waves. He came and sat beside her. She felt herself grow rigid as he put his arm round her shoulders. His lips touched her ear as he spoke, and her body, independent of her mind or emotions, yearned for him.

'If Charles Nightingale was still alive I could understand you still being frightened of trusting me,' he said. 'You would be right to be suspicious. He was a powerfully connected man. We would never have been able to get him. There are people we can't get. They are too well connected. They can pull too many strings. From paedophile MPs with expensive solicitors who turn up for police questioning, to people like Nightingale, too clever, too rich and too well connected to be done. I'm glad the bastard's dead. Please trust me, Stella.'

She turned to him and looked into his eyes. She wanted to trust him. She liked so much about him. She found him unbearably attractive, and knew that, with just an ounce of trust, she would find herself in love. But she had once loved

Colin, trusted him implicitly, and he had betrayed her. Faith, trust, love – if she were ever to feel these emotions again they would have to be fought for, the man proved worthy of the gifts. She kissed him.

'The ship leaves at five o'clock – that's in half an hour, John Smith,' she said with a smile. 'I'm going back to my cabin to sort out my work and have a quick cup of tea. Do you think, if you came to my cabin at six, we could make love and still arrive in time for second-sitting dinner?'

7

Father Peter stood on the adjacent hill to the Devil's Dyke and looked across at the vast expanse of Sussex countryside. The hill was seven hundred and eleven feet above sea level, and the air was fresh and biting cold. Down in Brighton the carbon monoxide levels were often quite dreadful as more and more people used the car instead of public transport. But even on a hot, still day there was usually a refreshing breeze up here.

He looked at Jack waiting in great anticipation, as a young man strapped to a hang-glider was preparing to leap from a ridge. Jack's face was flushed from the north-easterly wind.

'I'm glad you asked me to bring you up here, Father,' he said. 'I don't come up to the downs often enough. It's always the same, don't you think, that one doesn't make the most of the facilities in one's own home town? I often think this when I'm away in another place directing a play. I go exploring everywhere, museums, country walks – and yet, here in Brighton, let's see, it must be at least three years since Maureen and I came for a walk on the Dyke.'

He had such an open face, Father Peter thought. Maureen had obviously decided not to tell him anything. He wondered whether she ever would. Father Peter had not wanted his suspicions confirmed. He would have preferred to remain ignorant, like Jack – who still believed that his wife had once had a miraculous win on the roulette – rather than to have heard Maureen's confession, two days ago, and know the truth. The truth was that she had stolen the money from Jenny's safe aboard *Jester*, while her friend lay dead in the other part of the boat. Then, aided and abetted by Stella, she had laundered the money in a casino in Nice.

When she had made her confession, she told him that most of the details in her story had been true, and she had won some money. But the amount she had won was only the equivalent of five hundred pounds. Father Peter frowned as he remembered the list of events Maureen had told him. One of which Jack had once innocently referred to as an 'escapade.'

The wind changed direction and Jack shivered. 'Stella's enjoying eighty degrees in Miami, lucky thing. Maureen had a card from her this morning. It took five days to get here. She's got a wonderful job, don't you think, visiting all these exotic places? Goodness knows why she's giving it up to go to Warsaw.'

'I suppose she needs to understand the country she was told so much about as a child,' Father Peter said.

The young man on the hang-glider took a run forward and leapt into space. Jack had his mouth open as he watched the fellow manipulate the craft in the wind.

Father Peter thought about Stella. The poor little thing had borne this burden of secrecy for her friend. No wonder she wanted to get away from Brighton. He was appalled by all the fear and guilt she had been carrying during the last five years.

He walked on with Jack in silence, keeping to the sheep track, while watching the glider ride the air currents. He liked Jack's company. The remarkable thing about men, he thought, was their ability to share silence. Women always wanted to fill silence with conversation, when to share someone's quiet company was often far more reassuring.

140

He thought about what Maureen had told him during her confession. Because she had taken the back-street route to the harbour, avoiding the congestion on the seafront road, she had reached the Marina by seven-fifteen pm. That fateful night, she was desperately trying to prevent her house from being repossessed by the bank. She had parked her car and hurried to *Jester*, hoping that Jenny could be persuaded to lend her some money, which she would repay as soon as she could.

When she reached the motor yacht, Jenny was lying on the floor, her clothes all dishevelled. Maureen had turned her over, thinking she had fainted, and discovered she was dead. At first she was horrified and frightened. She immediately thought of going for help, but didn't want strangers to see Jenny as she was, so she had lifted her up on to the couch and straightened her clothes. Then she remembered Jenny saying that they always carried money on board – the interest from their off-shore accounts – in Deutsche marks, yen, dollars and sterling. This was the last chance Maureen had of saving her home. There was nothing more she could do to help Jenny, so Maureen had gone straight to the plush stateroom, where she knew the safe was hidden behind the mirror on Jenny's dressing-table. Maureen remembered Jenny saying that she would have to change the combination to the same one as the court security number. She tried the number and found that Jenny really had used the same one. Then she found an old Harrods plastic bag in a wardrobe, filled it with the money and left the boat quickly, knowing that she could still be almost invisible in the thick sea mist.

When she reached the safety of her car, she suddenly panicked about what she had done. She also feared that the police might think she had killed Jenny.

At that point during her confession, Father Peter had asked her whether she knew who had murdered Jenny. Maureen had thought for a while before whispering, 'I can't think who could have done such a terrible thing, Father.' She had driven to Stella's for help, and reached the flat at about seven-forty.

Stella had cried when Maureen told her of Jenny's death. Then she demanded to know every detail of how the body had appeared when she first saw it. Maureen had told her she remembered a lot of loose hair on the floor. It looked as if it had been pulled or twisted from Jenny's head. Almost as if she'd been tortured. She then told him that Stella suddenly took charge, calmed her down, took the money from her, and hid it in her own wardrobe. She then put some of the groceries she had bought from the supermarket into one of the two plastic carrier bags, in which she had just carried home her own shopping. She told Maureen she should take the bag to establish an alibi for her missing time. Maureen hurried home with the bag of shopping and Jack believed her when she said she had been lost and ended up in the supermarket.

Before Stella and Maureen travelled to Rome, they lined their suitcases with screwed-up banknotes. They pushed them into shoes, jumpers and everything they were carrying. They were terrified of being stopped by the customs officers at the airport, and were amazed that they managed to get the cases though safely.

After Stella had finished gathering all her research for the travel feature, they had travelled by train from Rome to Nice, booked into a hotel, then gone to the casino and changed all the money into chips. They meant to play just long enough to establish their presence without arousing any suspicion. The irony of the situation was, that because the casino management were trying to attract the Australian tourists, Maureen and Stella were allowed to keep winning. The unfortunate Australians had seen the piles of chips beside them and presumed they had won a fortune.

As soon as the Australians joined the tables, Stella decided

142

it was time to stop playing. When they eventually counted up the chips, they had five hundred pounds more than when they had started gambling. Enough, in fact, for Maureen to pay Stella back all the expenses she had laid out on her behalf. Maureen had received a cheque from the casino, made out in French francs. It was another alibi for her story about winning the money.

What evil can come about because of what people considered materialistic necessity, Father Peter thought with sadness. Stress, strain and illness. People killed themselves after losing money at Lloyd's, or for not registering a lottery ticket with the right number. Chance, achievement, social position, the loss of face – all materialism. And the priests kept trying, fighting even those within their own ranks, ready to compromise with evil. They kept offering redemption, trying to save souls.

'You don't realise what it's like, Father,' Maureen had said. 'I played by the rules, tried to improve myself, studied, worked hard. To find out that insurance companies don't have the same rules negates your whole life's worth. And Jenny . . . I paid my taxes, my national insurance – she didn't pay taxes on all that wealth. I realised that rules only applied to people like me – but not the rich, not the old-boy network that rules this country, the establishment that runs the banks and insurance companies. It's never ever been any different. I just believed the myth of democracy, and I was wrong.

'But, Father, I feel bad about dragging Stella into it all. And I don't feel the same person any more. I hate feeling bitter about society – I want to have faith in something again, to believe in people, and not to be a slave to cynicism. I suppose, Father, the house was the symbol of everything I'd ever aspired to be. I hated being looked down on when I was a child – being judged by where I lived. I remember those cruel words, 'And where do you live, Maureen?' – and feeling the fear that the friendliness would go and the

143

warmth and approval vanish as soon as I gave my address. And it did. My children take everything for granted, Father. I hear them describe other friends' homes, sometimes with pity, if the person lives in a flat like the one I was brought up in. Poverty, Father, is ugly. And when you're trapped and you can't see any way out . . . Oh Father, I understand why some of the kids these days get angry. Everything is fixed and arranged by the well-off. Judges, politicians, they're mostly all from privileged backgrounds. How can you 'get on your bike' when you never have the money to get one, and you don't know where to go, even if one is *given* to you?'

Thank God Maureen had returned to church, Father Peter thought. She had been as she was as a child: angry, but absolutely repentant. She had rediscovered the freedom through service to others. She had become reconciled with the faith again. Already her face had lost that hard, unhappy expression. He had introduced her to the new young priest, who would take over from him after Easter. She had started telling him some of Brighton's history. He had overheard her telling the young priest the legend of Devil's Dyke, in the same way that old Father John had told him, when he had just arrived in Brighton.

'Once upon a time, the devil began to dig a vast chasm so the sea could come in and swallow up all the churches and good people in the area. But an old lady, hearing the noise he made, lit a candle, and Old Nick, thinking it was the dawning sun, left his work unfinished.'

Father Peter paused for a while to catch his breath. He could see Chanctonbury Ring in the distance. The place where an old pre-Roman temple was supposed to be buried. Witches were known to dance there on their special nights. Once it had trees planted in a ring on the summit. Since the gales of 1987, the old place looked quite bald.

Back to 1987, always back to 1987, when Old Nick began to weave his mischief. It was in June 1987 that

Charles Nightingale got into financial trouble, when he lost a fortune in the value of his shares, after a false opinion poll rumour. His brother was killed in a motor accident shortly afterwards. In October 1987 the gales nearly destroyed Maureen's and Jack's house, which later involved them in fighting an insurance company. In 1987, young Joe Hennessy's foster father had died. He had been a wonderful influence on the boy. Without her husband, the wife was unable to cope with the young lad, and he had drifted into the wrong company.

He looked across towards the villages of Poynings and Saddlescombe. Despite the cold, changeable weather, lambs had been born. He could see them leaning against their mothers' woolly shapes. And, since 1987, he had experienced a recurring dream. Just once a year it came to him.

> *Friday night's dream,*
> *Saturday told,*
> *Will always come true,*
> *Be it ever so old.*

His mother had recited that to him when he was a boy. But this dream had never been dreamed on a Friday night. Not until last week. He now found himself haunted by the vividness of it.

He had been standing on a hill, just like the Devil's Dyke, holding Saint Mary Magdalene's hand. She was showing him fields of ripe corn. Suddenly the corn began to flatten into patterns of eight, weaving round and round until it was a circular rose.

He remembered the New Age people talking about aliens and the Earth Mother's natural energies, but he applied his powers of reason to alter his vision until he could focus his sight on the field. Then he saw that the patterns were caused

145

by the movement of sheep, following each other, head to tail. A perfectly natural occurrence.

Suddenly all the sheep panicked and fled from something in the middle of the circle. Slowly a black creature left the cornfield and walked up the hill towards him. The little black sheep had the saddest face, the most pitiful look. It was desperate for forgiveness. When he looked into the sheep's eyes, he recognised its soul. That soul asked forgiveness, desperately wanted to make the act of contrition, craved redemption and absolution.

'Do you fancy a cup of tea, Father?'

They turned back towards the public house at the top of the Dyke.

As they drew near to the carpark, he remembered Barry's story of the shooting, the taxi ordered for a John Smith, the two men waiting by the pub, and the men in the waiting car. Who were they? Was it possible that Charles had arranged to meet someone? If so, had the meeting come about as a result of receiving the faxed message at his home that morning? What if the men were with Charles waiting for the same person. Why would the men in the car parked further along, before the pub, come up so close behind the taxi? Perhaps they thought someone was arriving by car to see them. Or could it be that they were there to protect Charles from someone? Could they have been the police? But then it made no sense if the police called in the taxi-driver to look at mug shots. Were the men with Charles rogue police, or just men working for Charles trying to protect him? If so, from whom? Father Peter tried to imagine the night-time scene. As the men moved towards the taxi the gunshot had sounded. Someone must have been hiding, waiting for an opportunity to kill Charles. Could it have been the same person who ordered the taxi for John Smith? And how did the killer escape? Perhaps he didn't run westwards but circled the back of the pub. The

146

track would have led him, if he crossed a gully, into the back of a small carpark. From there he could have driven down into Poynings and then towards Worthing, avoiding the main roads. He would have to be pretty fit to escape so quickly.

'I'm going to the West Country soon, Father,' Jack said as he brought a tray of tea over to the table. 'I hope the weather will be OK. I'm directing *A Midsummer Night's Dream*. It's a lovely play to do.'

Father Peter started to laugh. 'You will never believe this Jack, but I once played Titania. I remember my brothers teasing me unmercifully. It was performed, I'm afraid, rather like Edith Evans with a breaking voice. I was about thirteen I think.'

Jack elaborated on his ideas for the production, and the actors he wanted to play the parts.

Father Peter was suddenly overwhelmed by remorse for not being a little gentler towards Maureen when telling her to make the sacrament of penance. He should have been more forgiving, he decided. Only this morning he had been wandering around his own room, listening to the children shouting in the playground below, and had suddenly felt very lost. He had thought, prayed and meditated for so long in his room that it was now almost a part of him. His home, the place where he kept his few precious personal things, and where he sat with his memories. How dared he lecture Maureen? The woman had been desperate to keep her home. Perhaps she was also being kinder by sheltering Jack from the truth, to let him dream in innocence, so he could lose himself in Shakespeare, rather than fret with the shared guilt of theft. As Jack rambled on, his thoughts drifted towards his impending retirement.

He would miss all his friends when he eventually retired to Spain. Especially Mike O'Reilly. When he told Mike he would be leaving Saint Mary Magdalene's for Marbella,

Mike had said, 'I'll write to some AA members in the area, Father, and tell them that there's a priest arriving with a sense of humour. Then you can have some of them come to confession. They'll give you better stories to listen to than the moans of a few old ex-pats, don't you think, Father? At least they'll give you some hairy confessions.'

A sense of humour? Did Mike really think he had a sense of humour? Sometimes, these days, he felt so sad that a laugh seemed beyond his reach. The person who always used to make him laugh was Tad. He was just about the most irreverent, blasphemous man he had ever known. No wonder Stella was such a little toughie, he thought with amusement, with a father like Tad.

'Yes, I thought it was funny too,' Jack said, relieved at seeing his smile.

Father Peter wondered what on earth Jack had been saying to him. All the way back in the car he listened for a clue, so he could understand why Jack had been so pleased that he smiled. He was none the wiser when they parted. But Jack was happy enough.

'See you soon, Father,' he said, as he dropped Father Peter off at the church.

He felt tired after supper. The young priest was so full of ideas, plans and dreams for the future that it took every ounce of his diminishing energy to keep pace with the conversation. Like an old bear, he crept up the stairs, back to his room and the blessed peace of his own company.

He sat by his window looking again through Bessie's diary. It was a mild, still night. The wind had dropped during supper and he could hear all the movements in the town.

He decided that he must give Bessie's envelope to Stella soon. Bessie had left it to his discretion when to give it to her. Now he felt the time was right. She could have it when she returned from the cruise.

He opened the window slightly. The air was quite warm. What strange weather, he thought. One minute blowing a gale, the next as muggy as a night in Hong Kong. He had even seen a couple of mosquitos earlier. Mosquitos in March. He wondered whether it was to do with all the hot water in the drains. He had seen some on the way to the post office first thing this morning. They were hovering by the entrance to the supermarket.

An idea was trying to form in his brain. Supermarket. Maureen had told him that the night she had gone to see Jenny, Stella had said she had just returned from the supermarket. Which one? If it was the supermarket she usually used, it was down by the Marina. That meant she must have been down there at the same time as the killer. Jenny had telephoned Stella and found she was out, then she had called Maureen just before seven and phoned Charles *at* seven. Maureen had reached the marina by seven-fifteen. If Stella had been shopping there, she might have caught sight of the killer. It was very possible she had seen him. But, even if she recognised him at the time, she could not have known he was about to murder Jenny. But what about later? If he feared that she suspected him of murder, would he not try to contact her, to see if she knew anything? Then Stella, too, would have been in danger that year.

He looked up. The moon was bulging into an almost straining protrusion against the black sky. It wasn't a full moon. He had never seen it such a strange shape. It should have been a half moon, not this elongated, extended light. Was it his imagination or was the dark side flecked with red?

Tad would have loved this mysterious moon, he thought, remembering his nights staring down Tad's telescope at a moon much closer to the earth than usual. He smiled. Tad would come out with all sorts of strange bits of information. So many nights they had laughed together. When she was a teenager Stella would listen while they discussed their war experiences, interrupting with, 'And then what happened, Dad?' or, 'And what did you do then, Father?'

He stared at the moon. How he missed his old friend. When he had first arrived at Liverpool docks, Tad had told him, laughing loudly, 'The water round the ship was full of plink, plonk, splosh, you know.' They had drunk some vodka and Father Peter had been convulsed by the cartoon images of plink, plonk, splosh, as an introduction to Britain. Tad told him, 'The authorities, they come on ship to see if any soldiers have kept their guns. Everyone was told to hand them in you see. So, Father, everyone who had not given up their gun – overboard, plink, plonk, splosh. There were probably enough guns in Liverpool docks to start another war.'

Father Peter suddenly sat up straight in his chair, remembering the next part of the conversation. How could he have been so stupid to have forgotten?

Tad had been laughing, clutching his sides. Then he'd leaned forward conspiratorially, 'But not this monkey, Peter. Potocki was cunning. I stick my Luger down my underpants. I make bloody sure it's not loaded. Don't want to shoot my bloody cock off. I think if anyone search me, they think I'm a bloody Polish queer.'

Father Peter felt the beginnings of a headache spread from between his eyes, across to his right temple and then into his upper molars as he remembered what he asked him. 'Did you really keep it, Tad?'

'You bloody bet, Father,' he said. 'I swop my rifle for the Luger. This other Pole, he take it from a dead German officer. Course I bloody keep it. Who knows if another war comes? Who knows if those bloody Russians don't get cheeky again? The Poles and the Russians have always fought. If they ever got here, I would join the guerrillas. I keep it in the attic. Safe so no one knows. I wrap the bullets in the greaseproof paper. They will last for years like that.'

Father Peter sat with his head in his hands, the tears dripping on to Bessie's Filofax. He had prayed to the Boss for understanding. But the pain, the sorrow of understanding, was so great. To understand what poverty, anger, loss of faith in justice could do – the fear of so many souls, the temptations of those who had been favoured. How could he, an old priest, begin to understand? To begin to understand the sins of the world would mean longing for the peace of death. He had just about begun to understand his own hidden fears. And that understanding, with his quest for truth, was leading him straight into his dream, to the little black sheep.

8

It was her last night aboard the *QE2*, and in the Princess Grill Dining Room someone called Bill was celebrating his birthday. The head waiter, his assistant and several other members of the dining room staff had gathered round the table to sing *Happy Birthday*.

Stella watched the proud birthday boy – all of sixty – trying to blow out the discreetly arranged candles on the cake, and smiling gratefully, as his wife tried to help him from the opposite side of the table. The combined marital exhalations extinguished the flames, enabling Bill to have his wish. Placing his fingers to his lips, he blew a kiss to his beaming wife.

Stella smiled at the memory of John Smith's elaborate demonstration of blowing her a kiss when she had seen him off at Miami Airport.

'We will meet again,' he said, 'if only to play chess. You might find me waiting for you at Southampton.'

'Well,' she had replied, 'it would be useful to have someone to help me with the luggage.'

He had laughed. *'Tu eres muy traviesa.* A man could never be bored with you. He would never understand you or know you. You would always be an enigmatic labyrinth of intentions.'

She wondered whether he would be there, waiting in Southampton docks tomorrow morning when she disembarked.

Stella was sharing a port-side window table with five other people: a couple of journalists, one popular author of crime fiction, a political writer and a TV soap celebrity. She had enjoyed being on the table, listening to all their observations about the trip.

'The British *QE2* cruising experience is where la-di-da meets hi-dee-hi,' one of the other journalists, a witty man called Frank, remarked, after the three of them had been given a tour of the ship by the Cunard public relations officer.

Frank delighted in making Stella laugh hysterically whenever he thought she was being too serious. As they were being conducted round the ship and were shown first the gymnasium on deck seven, and then the Thalasso therapy pool on deck six, he announced in a mock northern voice, 'I think it's a bit disgusting myself, the way all those people angle their bodies against those jets of water.'

He had managed to keep up a non-stop banter as they were shown the engine room and the kitchens. They finally ended up on the bridge, where Stella was asked if she would like to blow the noon test whistle. Frank's comments threatened to make the whistle late as Stella collapsed in a giggling heap, unable even to purse her lips, let alone form her mouth into a controlled shape to blow the whistle. Frank then blew it with a great sense of satisfaction.

She agreed with him. The *QE2* could be either like a genteel country house hotel – with soft piano music in the cosy, wood-panelled Chart Room Bar, the faint strains of a symphony orchestra to be heard in the Crystal Bar, the interesting lectures in the theatre, and delicate afternoon teas in the Queen's Grill Lounge – or a livelier place catering for those who wanted gambling, bingo, the cinema, dancing, floor shows with comedians to make you laugh, and the warm jazz-filled atmosphere of the Golden Lion British pub.

Stella kept out of the gambling area – it reminded her too much of the fear and terror she'd experienced in attempting to launder Maureen's stolen money. She still marvelled at how they had got away with it. After they had returned to Brighton, she and Maureen had made a pact. They swore never to tell anyone, except by mutual consent if either of them wished to confess to Father Peter.

It was the stolen money that had confused the police assigned to Jenny's murder, John Smith had told her. He confided that at first they had suspected that Father Peter had killed her in a passionate frenzy. But forensic tests soon proved the theory wrong. They had also suspected Robert Allan for a while, but his alibi for the time she was murdered was absolutely beyond doubt. John Smith had given Stella the information she needed to get a better picture of the fishing quota mystery.

Apparently, in 1987, just after Charles Nightingale's brother was killed in a car accident, the brother's widow came to the police with the story that Charles had arranged her husband's accident because of a row over arrangements Charles wanted to make with the fishing fleet. Within days of making her statement she retracted it, sold her house and moved abroad. There was nothing the crime squad could prove about the man's death. The circumstances were suspicious. The accident had taken place on a deserted road in Kent with no other vehicle involved, and the brother had died from a broken neck, which had been presumed to be the result of crashing into a tree.

Charles had a good alibi for that evening. He had been dining with a high-ranking civil servant.

Miraculously, Charles managed to double the fleet's profits, so that he continued to live in the same lavish lifestyle that he had enjoyed before the shares disaster. Tax probes revealed nothing. Some of the best police economists were employed to look into his affairs, but everything on paper was legitimate, and they were soon told to drop the enquiry. Then the drug squad was tipped off by Interpol about an American using ships to bring drugs from Colombia into Britain, through Kent. But again, all officers watching the fleets at Hastings found nothing.

A police officer, who attended the same Freemasons' lodge as a British Telecom engineer, was told that Charles Nightingale had wanted to know who was making nuisance calls to his home, and had been given the information. The engineer was gossiping about Jenny. The police already knew that Jenny had been making the calls, but they had not caught her ringing from the same telephone the right number of times to warrant bringing charges. When Jenny was found murdered, the same policeman who had talked to the Telecom engineer became suspicious and reported the conversation to the inspector in charge of the murder enquiry. But again all police enquiries revealed that Charles had an alibi for every moment of that evening.

It was also known that he was about to be made chairman of the bench, and was also being considered for a knighthood. John Smith had interviewed Charles but could only surmise that Charles had probably had an affair with Jenny but there was no information that could prove he had murdered her.

Stella had made notes on what John Smith had told her so she could help Father Peter understand. That was what the dear old man wanted, to understand, and she was determined that he should.

Pieces of Bill's cake were being offered to everyone in the dining-room. Stella declined the thick slice of cream-filled chocolate cake. She had already put on weight. The food on the QE2 was just too good, and too easily available. Every time she thought of her departure to Warsaw, she had helped herself to a little bit of this or another bit of that, knowing she was saying goodbye to this kind of luxury food for the next three years, with the result that her jeans were now quite tight round the stomach.

She had enjoyed listening to the writers give their pre-book-signing talks, especially the crime-writer, who looked more like a retired schoolmistress than someone who dealt with poisoning and garroting, murder and mayhem. They had coffee together one morning in the quiet Queen's Grill Lounge. Stella had been telling her about her short stay in Bal Harbour, in Miami Beach, just after her three-day American cruise, and was explaining how, despite the British and German tourists' fears about visiting Miami, she had felt safe there, when shopping in the famous Bal Harbour Shopping Mall or walking along the beach. This was because she knew there was so much security in the area.

This led to a discussion about the American right to bear arms. She was quite suprised to hear the old lady defend the idea, and also to argue that people should have the right to defend their homes and property with the gun if necessary.

Stella had thought about the discussion later, wondering whether Bessie and Jenny would still be alive if the British had been able to have the right to bear arms. But then, she reasoned with herself, who is ever expecting a predator before being murdered? Jennie had welcomed the killer aboard and Bessie had invited the killer into the house. They weren't expecting violence. She thought about it again at night, while she enjoyed the security of walking at any time in the early hours, alone on deck, knowing she was safe from any mugger or killer. For a woman this aspect of the cruise was very important, to be able to be alone, free to enjoy the night air, to be part of the whole movement of the sea and sky without fear.

She enjoyed listening to the cruise director's interview with the soap star about her career. It took place in the Grand Lounge. The actress gave a good performance. She was confident and humorous when answering questions from the audience. It was only when she realised that Stella was not a show-business journalist and was in no way interested in writing a story about her, that she relaxed and allowed Stella to see the more real, serious and very vulnerable woman hidden behind the smiling actor's mask.

Tomorrow they would be docking in Southampton. Five hours after the passengers disembarked, the ship would be ready to sail again, back to New York.

Stella was glad she was arriving home in time for Easter, and that she had a few weeks before leaving for Warsaw. She was looking forward to wearing some comfortable old clothes again. She had dressed up more on the cruises than she had in her whole life.

She had prefered the *QE2* cruise to the American one. She had managed to catch up with all the new films in the air-conditioned cinema, she had listened every evening to the jazz, attended a variety of talks in the theatre, and plundered the vast library and reading-room.

Often she would wander around the ship at night, always stopping at the mammoth ship's puzzle, trying to find the right-shaped piece, then when returning later she would find someone else had found the elusive bit and used it to further develop the picture.

Wherever she strolled, she always ended up in the Grand Lounge, where a stand-up comedian, his face perspiring with exertion, would be reducing the audience to howls of laughter. Stella loved his humour. Sometimes there were coarse, booze-and-bottoms jokes. Sometimes he made clever, witty digs at British politicians. She would stand at the back of the lounge enjoying the sheer wonder of the noise of people's hilarity.

The greatest asset people had was their sense of humour, she thought. It was humour that saved the world from despair. Satire could destroy despots. She wondered whether perhaps mankind had been put on the world to make God laugh. Only sometimes it turned out to be a cruel joke. In a way, she mused, she had played an esprit de corps, on John Smith. She grinned as she thought about it, about how she had inflicted on him her sense of facetiousness.

She had told him everything he had wanted to know, after they had made love, and while they were sharing a post-coital shower. She had then wrapped herself in a towel, placed a flannel on her head impersonating a barrister's wig, and then in her most pompous plummy voice said, 'And of course, m'lud, this officer, having inveigled his way into the defendant's affections, so that the poor woman would do or say anything to continue this passionate affair, is guilty of the most cynical case of entrapment, and all charges against the defendant should be dismissed. May I suggest, m'lud, that the evidence a sexually aroused female gives while being kissed under a warm, soothing shower, is totally inadmissable. As the unfortunate, weeping lady told me later, m'lud, "It was the orgasm what did it, sir."'

John Smith had emerged from behind the plastic curtain with a look of absolute disbelief. 'You cunning little bitch,' he said, 'I think I love you.'

During her nightly prowls round the deck, she would stop and chuckle whenever she remembered the moment.

People were exchanging addresses, thanking the waiters and stewards. The holidays were over and, as one journalist said, 'Ah well, after tomorrow, it's back to the Marmite and toast for breakfast.'

Photographs were taken of the special friends made during the voyage. Last drinks were taken in the bars. Groups lingered over coffee, last waltzes were danced, shipboard romances were painfully ended, and the laughter in the Grand Lounge was the last gasp of abandoned mirth before departure.

*   *   *

The corridors were lined with people's luggage, all in neat piles outside their cabins. By twelve midnight they would be collected and taken down to the hold, where they would be unloaded as soon as the ship docked.

Stella struggled with her own bags, trying to squeeze into the case the odd bargain she had picked up in America. Everything was clean except for the dress she had worn that evening. Her skirts and slacks had been beautifully laundered by the Chinese laundry down in the bowels of the ship. One passenger told her that he always arrived on board with his cleaning and then handed it straight in to the steward. He was part of a select band of rich eccentric travellers who regularly enjoyed at least three cruises a year on the QE2.

There were others who had saved for years to enjoy the wonderful experience, couples who had retired, whose insurance policies had matured, and who were doing absolutely everything together. There were some old ones whose children had clubbed together to send them on a voyage, and there were bands of old grannies, travelling together, and living each day in a frenzy of activity. It was usually these old girls whom Stella bumped into on her nightly prowls. They were always finishing the midnight meal, laid on for those who became hungry at night.

The luggage had all been placed in the covered area of the docks. As she walked over to claim her two large suitcases, she saw him. He was standing talking to two customs officers. As soon as he caught sight of her he strolled over. He was looking serious. Her heart thumped. Had she totally misjudged the whole affair? When he spoke her knees felt weak.

'Stella Potocki, I'm arresting you' – he paused, and her stomach dropped somewhere in the vicinity of her feet – 'for interfering with a police officer in the course of his duty, and then causing undue distress to said police officer by not continuing to do same. You do not have to say anything but if you do not mention now something which you later use in your defence, this cop may decide that your failure to mention it now strengthens the case against you.' He grinned at her.

She hit him hard in the chest. 'That was a really shitty thing to do,' she said, breathless with rage.

'Now you're assaulting a police officer,' he laughed, 'and I've even cleaned the car out to escort you in style.'

'I'll forgive you if you carry the cases.'

When he kissed her, the world spun round as if she were about to faint.

'I love you Stella Potocki,'

'I love you too, John Smith.'

9

The grey clouds that heralded Good Friday had arrived, and hung ready to disgorge what his mother always called 'God's tears'. For the last hour one confession had followed another as the great purging for souls began before Easter. As Jesus had instructed the apostle Peter, so he as a priest was to forgive the one who wronged Him not seven times but seventy times seven. The baptised person who sins again can never be beyond redemption and, provided he repents, the sinner must be forgiven, so he can be reconciled with the Father once more.

Father Peter was the intermediary between the penitents and God. During the last sixty minutes he had listened to remorse over sex, money, people not getting their own way, anger, sibling rivalry, gossip – all human fears and pettiness, shame and despair. The church was humming with the whispered penances from all those who had admitted, confessed and repented their sins. But still the one for whom he waited had not arrived. He reached under the folds of his robe for the letter in his pocket. It had been posted from Wales and had arrived in the mail this morning. While he waited for the next confession he read it once more.

Dear Father Peter,

I hope you received the Filofax I sent you in February. This letter is being posted by one of the lads in the Welch

Fusiliers, who is being sent back home. I thought it would be quicker than trying for weeks to get it out from here.

I am working with the Red Cross in Bosnia. They are a great bunch of people and I think we are doing some very good work. But sometimes we get scared. That is why I sent you the Filofax. It was getting a bit hectic and I thought something might happen to me. I wanted you to know. I also wanted you to understand.

I had to leave, Father. I had to run away. Perhaps I was wrong but at the time I thought nobody would believe that I was innocent. I never ever committed murder. Not ever. That's the truth. But I did steal Miss Baker's Filofax and her credit cards. I was stupid. I did it because I was bored. It was hot and I was banned from going into the centre of Brighton or anywhere near the arcades because I'd been done for strimming. You know, I'd drilled through a coin, put some fishing line through it, put the coin into a fruit machine and jiggled it until the mechanism knocked up ten quids worth of credit. And then they caught me. Well, I suppose it does ruin the machines but I don't know, at the time, I thought they'd had a lot of money from me that summer. I suppose it was a bit like scrumping.

Well, Miss Baker was Chairman of the court that banned me. I was on conditional bail for three weeks waiting to have some probation reports prepared. That Friday, I was up on Race Hill about six o'clock. I could hear all the sounds of life coming from the pier. I knew all my friends were in Brighton and I felt fed up. So I started to walk and just kept walking.

The next thing was, I found myself looking at a row of houses with front gardens, and I could see the evening paper sticking out of one front door. So I wandered round the back and saw the small kitchen window was open. I just jiggled the catch and I was in. I helped myself to some

*cold beer and then I saw the Filofax and her picture on
the sideboard. I suppose I thought it was a really funny
coincidence.*

*Father, I know now that what I did was wrong. It
was a sin. I stole. For that action I'm truly sorry. And
for all the things that happened because of what I did
I'm sorry. But because of the pictures I found a month
later, in the back flap of the Filofax, I honestly believe I
was meant to take it. I left one picture for you to find.
Perhaps you don't remember, but that little toy dog in
the picture was mine.*

Father Peter let the letter rest in his lap while he straightened
his neck against the wall. 'Perhaps you don't remember
. . .' Of course he remembered. When little Joe Hennessy
first turned up at Saint Mary Magdalene's primary school
clutching the dog in his arms, he had thought the dog
resembled the one he had bought for Bessie's son. He had
watched the boy when he was running round the playground
and noticed that he had Bessie's wide grin and open blue
eyes. He had talked to Mrs Hennessy about her son and
had been told he was adopted. His suspicions confirmed,
every time Bessie cried on his shoulder he was able to tell
her with honesty that he was able to keep in touch with the
family and he knew the boy was being brought up well.

His neck having stretched enough to receive the desired
click, Father Peter returned to the letter.

*I sold the credit cards an hour after I left, for two hundred
pounds, and then I went back to where I was staying. It
was on Saturday, when I saw the police coming up the
road and thought someone had given me away, that I ran
for it. I read the paper on Monday and realised they'd
send me down for committing burglary while I was on
bail. My friend Jim helped me. Do you remember we were*

165

best friends at school? He hid me in the shed at the bottom
of his garden. Then he applied for a temporary passport
from the post office. We put my picture in it and I went
over to France from Newhaven. I got the train to Paris
and then posted the passport back to him so he didn't get
into trouble.

We kept in touch and when he told me about the
murders I thought of coming back. I was going to get
in touch with you for help. Then when I heard the police
were holding you as a possible suspect I didn't know what
to do, so I just kept on the move.

Say a prayer for me please Father.

Yours sincerely,
Joe Hennessy. (I'm
known here as Pierre.)

He had called himself Peter. Was it after his old priest
who had known his secret? Father Peter wondered. His
eyes began to fill. He tried to fight his lachrymal mood
by neatly folding the letter and replacing it in his pocket.
He had asked the Boss for understanding. What strange
twist of fate had led Bessie to sit in judgement on her
own son, for Joe to steal his own mother's Filofax, giving
Jenny the excuse to indulge in idle, mischief-making nuisance calls? Father Peter could understand the pain of
Joe's guilt.

How terrible the boy must have felt thinking that his theft
had led to his own mother's murder. What fear must he
have experienced while on the move in France? Why had
it all happened? The old priest contemplated the pattern of
events that had led one young boy to the discovery of his
own identity.

The little toy dog from the Red Cross bazaar bought with
love for his friend Bessie's illegitimate child had given the
boy and him the truth. Love equals truth. An act of love

must bring about a truth. A good. And now the boy was doing good for the Red Cross, helping others.

'Bless me Father for I have sinned. It is nearly five years since my last confession.'

It was the voice he had been expecting, Stella's voice. He took a deep breath and leaned back in his chair. He could hear her gathering together pieces of paper. This was going to take some time. He sighed and then said, 'Make your confession.'

'I have committed murder, Father.'

He closed his eyes. For a moment he felt dizzy. His ribs were hurting but he said, 'This is a truly dreadful mortal sin. Who did you murder?'

'I shot Charles Nightingale, Father. I had to do it before he killed me, and because I knew he killed Bessie and Jenny.'

'How could you be so positive that Charles had killed Bessie and Jenny?'

'Because Bessie and I had joked together. It was because we were frightened at what we had discovered about the drugs and the fish. When Sam died we weren't sure whether it had been an accident or murder, so we used to call Charles – just between ourselves – we used to call him the shark. Silly and childish really, but we were like scared children, fearful of the bogeyman. Anyway, we made a pact, that if either of us was attacked by him, or were unable to speak for some reason or other, because of a threat from him, we would draw the sign of the fish. Father, when I found Bessie's body she had drawn the sign of the fish in her own blood. The police might have suspected you because of its association with Christianity, but that sign was left for me, as a warning that it was Charles who killed her. So I knew who her murderer was, but I couldn't tell anyone. I didn't know who to trust. I also knew that in a court of law the fact Bessie had drawn a fish in her own blood could only be circumstantial evidence, relying on my testimony. And that I may or may not have been believed if my evidence was demolished by a good barrister.'

She let out a long half sobbed sigh. 'Father, the night Jenny was killed, I had been over to Bessie's brother Mark's house, in Bognor. Her other brother John and her two sisters were there as well. Because of my depression after Bessie's funeral, I hadn't done any basic shopping. I got home from Mark's about six-thirty in the evening, and by the time I'd changed into my old clothes I realised I had no coffee, milk, bread or fruit or any of the basic foods. So I grabbed my bag and walked down to the the Marina. I set off from my flat at six-fifty. At six-fifty-two Jenny called me, told me what time she'd called, and left her apology and confession about the nuisance calls. Unaware of her call, I continued walking down to the Marina. I entered the car park on the way to the supermarket. It was then about seven. That's when I saw Charles's Jag. He was sitting in the car and speaking on the mobile phone. Because I was frightened that he might have found out it was me who sent the photos to the police, I crept round the carpark avoiding any chance of him seeing me. I came out of the supermarket at ten past seven and saw that Charles's Jag was empty. I looked around carefully to make sure I was safe and hurried back up the cliffway.

'I was just coming along the pavement to my block of flats when I saw Charles's car further along the coast road. I don't know why I felt I had to, but I looked at my watch, and it was just after seven-fifteen. He was driving towards Rottingdean.

'When I got back into my flat, I emptied out the groceries, put the kettle on for a cup of tea and then made a sandwich. Then I went towards the lounge and saw that the answerphone light inside my study was blinking. It must have been about seven thirty-five by then. There were two messages from Jenny. The first, at six-fifty-two and then another at seven-o-seven. She told me Maureen

168

had forgiven her and was coming over to see her, and that she thought Charles had forgiven her because he had just phoned her back and asked if he could see her on her own. And then—' Stella's voice broke and Father Peter could hear the stifled sobs.

'Take your time now,' he said, trying to control his own breathing.

'And then she said, "It's all right, Stella, I can see Charles coming up the gangplank. I'll phone you later." I knew she could possibly have been in danger, but I also knew that he had already left the Marina – I'd seen him driving along the coast road. I was about to call to see if she was all right when Maureen arrived. And as you know, she had found the body by then.'

She paused and blew her nose. 'It was then, Father, after Maureen had gone home, that I knew he had to be stopped. I had the tape that proved he was with Jenny but I didn't want to give it to the police in case it incriminated Maureen. She had to save her home, and I know Jenny would have lent her the money. I also knew Charles would probably come for me next if he realised that Jenny was not with Sam in the boat and knew nothing about the drugs. From how Maureen described Jenny's body, it sounded as if she'd been tortured. I suppose I thought of it as war. A war for justice.

'I got Dad's old Luger out of my cupboard, found the bullets and kept it loaded in case he came to the flat. I was frightened, Father. Three people had been murdered and I didn't want to die with a broken neck or a slit throat. Later that night, when I'd had time to think more clearly, I decided to go to the police instead, and make a statement. I thought I could try to edit the tape so I wouldn't be incriminating Maureen, but then I heard on the radio that you had been arrested. The whole situation was so ludicrous and I was so angry, I decided to go ahead with my original plan to get Charles.

'First thing the next morning, I got up early and typed a message to Charles. I then went to a small newsagent in Rottingdean where I knew there was a fax machine. They were very busy so I told them I could operate it myself. I told them it was only one sheet of ten-by-eight to a local number. I dialled Charles's number at home and faxed the message. The message said, 'I have evidence of your connection with drugs and the murders of Bessie Baker and Jennifer Allan. Unless you bring two thousand pounds to the Devil's Dyke pub at twenty-three hundred hours tonight, I shall give all evidence to the police. I shall arrive by car at twenty-three hundred hours. If you are not there I will drive straight to the police.'

'I made my plans carefully. I drove back into Brighton, went to a telephone box in the Steyne and rang a private car-hire firm that I knew, because I'd seen it didn't have a taxi light on the roof. I arranged for the driver to pick up a Mr John Smith from the Dyke public house promptly at eleven o'clock that night because Mr Smith had to get a flight from Gatwick. I knew the driver would turn up for a good fare, and that it would fool Charles into thinking that the person who had sent the fax was driving the car, arriving at the pub on time for the meeting. I planned on being there earlier, because I anticipated that Charles wouldn't come on his own, but have some sort of back-up to help him. I was right.

'That Tuesday night, I arrived at ten o'clock and parked behind some bushes near a gate to a field. I wore the same dark clothes and balaclava I wore to go on the trip with Sam. I slipped across the road, circled the rear of the public house, and waited, lying on the ground, just over the lip of the hill. I was terrified, Father. I knew I would get the chance of one shot and it had to be accurate. I also knew that I had no family to disgrace if I was caught later and charged with murder. By half past ten the pub carpark was

170

full. At ten-forty-five I heard three cars approaching. One stopped short of the pub. I heard the men inside shout to the others, so I knew they were part of his back-up team. Then the other car parked opposite the pub doorway, and Charles's Jag drew up beside the corner of the carpark. He was obviously giving himself a clear eyeline for what he expected to be someone arriving by car.

'I nearly gave up my plans then. There were at least four men to help him as far as I could see. I couldn't see how I could possibly get away with it and escape safely. Then I thought of Bessie and Jenny and I got so angry that I didn't care any more.

'Charles had the driver's window wound down and was smoking. I edged along the ground, still on my stomach, until I was level with the Jag, and waited for the taxi to arrive. I knew that if they were expecting the person to come by car they might walk towards it and then I would have ten seconds at the most to shoot and run. At five to eleven I saw the taxi's headlights against the sky as it turned along the last part of Dyke Road to the pub. Charles threw his cigarette out of the window ready to confront the driver. My heart was pounding so loudly I felt sure he could hear me. Then I saw the two men near the pub door move towards the approaching taxi. I waited until Charles's eyes were fixed on the taxi, then I moved fast to the side of the Jag. He looked straight at me. Then I shot him. Oh, God.'

She stopped talking and blew her nose again.

Father Peter felt his own tears streaming down his face. He had looked at the faces of young Germans when he had pulled the trigger, felt sick with the act of killing, prayed as he shot men.

Stella continued, 'I didn't know I was capable of running as fast as I did. I thought the men would come after me. I ran round the back of the pub, and to my surprise both cars took off. As soon as I saw their rear lights disappear, I slipped quickly back across the road to my car. I heard the taxi reverse, the door slam and the taxi man return to the pub, so I presumed he'd spotted something. I took off my boots quickly, put them in a bag, and drove off through Poynings, and across the back of the downs, heading west. I found a quiet lay-by, put some sandals on I'd kept in the car, then got out, pulled my balaclava off, removed my jeans and sweater, put on a dress, and then put all the clothes I'd removed, with the gun, into the same bag as my boots. I returned to Brighton from Shoreham, stopping once at a garage to wash the wheels of my car. I dropped the boots, one by one, and the clothes, into a number of skips I'd seen earlier, outside different private houses and offices around Hove and Brighton.'

'What have you done with the gun, Stella?'

She was silent.

'Have you still got the gun?'

'No, Father. Later that week I threw it off Westminster Bridge, just by the Houses of Parliament. I said prayers for Charles Nightingale's soul, prayers for Bessie, Jenny, Sam and my father, and . . .' She paused. 'And I said a prayer for Guy Fawkes.'

His heart ached as he said, 'To be reconciled does not mean that you should avoid the due process of law, Stella. You must tell the police. I must know that it is your intention before I give you absolution.'

She was silent again.

Then she said, 'I have told a policeman, Father.'

'You have told him everything?'

'I have told him that I shot Charles Nightingale, Father.'

From the back of the church, he watched her head bowed in prayer, and thought of the cell in which he had worked out his own truths. Must this child, his first baptised, be

172

incarcerated? He offered up a prayer for her, for some miracle that would save her from prison.

She knelt before him waiting to take communion. His eyes were misty as she prepared for the body and blood. She had confessed and repented for having committed the mortal sin of murder. How many more people, often good caring citizens, were becoming so angry with lack of justice and insane ideologies that they were willing to risk imprisonment for executing their own, what they saw as, moral justice? The anger he had wanted to understand was as strong and as destructive as the hurricane of 1987. What damage would it do to society?

He caught her arm as she was leaving after mass. 'Wait for me, Stella. I have something for you.'

Her face was solemn as she waited obediently outside the church.

'Come with me Stella,' he said. 'Bessie left you an envelope which I was to give to you. I want you to have it now.'

She followed him into the sacristy and waited while he went to his room to fetch it. When he returned, he took her into the study where he sat her down and gave her the letter. He knew what it contained. It was Bessie's secret, about the child she had borne.

As Stella read the letter he watched the growing expression of amazement on her face. 'I have a half-brother,' she gasped.

Father Peter had known the boy's father had been Tadeusz. It was after Halina died that Bessie and Tad had their affair. Father Peter suspected that Bessie had always loved Tad but tried very hard to suppress her feelings. He remembered her confession of coveting another woman's husband, and crying while she told him, remembered the endless penances she had made for her sin. Then when

Halina died she had suddenly blossomed, and given up confession for some time.

Tad had never known about the child. That was how Bessie had wanted it to be. 'I love him but I don't want to marry him, Father. I couldn't live with him – he's too demanding,' she had told him.

'Do you know where he is Father?' Stella asked.

'Yes I do. I also know what poor Bessie could not know, and that was that Joe Hennessy was her son.'

'Joe Hennessy?' Stella thought for a while. 'You mean the boy who went missing?'

'Yes, he was the person who took the Filofax. The boy who Bessie had once judged in court was her son. Life is strange Stella, isn't it? Joe found out who his mother was, because he stole from her, and found some photographs tucked in the back wallet.'

'Do you know where is he now, Father?'

'He's working for the Red Cross in Bosnia. He's calling himself Pierre. Do I have your permission to let him know he has a sister?'

'But of course.' Her voice was the same pitch as that of an excited child. 'I can help him. I can get a good solicitor to sort out his bail offence and all the other problems so he can return here if he wants to.'

Father Peter took hold of her hand. 'Well, dear, what about yourself? I think before you start planning Joe's life, you have some more immediate problems of your own. When does your case come up?'

'Pardon?'

'When does your trial start? And do you think you will be allowed to stay out on bail?'

'Oh, Father, I'm not going to trial.'

'But you have confessed to the police.' 'No, Father, I said I told a policeman, and I did. But his evidence would be useless in a court of law.'

'I don't understand.'

She was blushing as she said, 'The situation when I confessed my crime to him could be seen by the defence to be an unacceptable means of entrapment. The reason I confessed to him under those circumstances was because I have no faith in the justice system, Father. I find it corrupt and the antithesis of every concept of law and order.'

Father Peter was stunned into silence. Stella was fidgeting with the letter and looking very ashamed. He looked at her sternly. 'What did he say when you told him?'

She swallowed nervously and replied, 'Among other things, he said "I think I love you."'

Father Peter looked at her. She squirmed uncomfortably under his gaze. 'The setting for terms of endearment have certainly changed since I was a young man,' he said with disdain. She blushed again and fiddled with Bessie's letter. Father Peter took a deep breath. 'Who is this policeman?'

The corners of her mouth began to dimple with suppressed laughter. People's natures really did not change from those they possessed as children, he thought. He had seen that same expression on Stella's face when Jenny or Maureen urged her into wickedness in class. She swallowed and tried to control herself. 'His name is John Smith, Father – I had no idea when I used the name to get the taxi to the Dyke pub that a policeman with the same name was working on the drugs case. It's strange, Father, don't you think?'

Yes it was strange. The whole insane mystery was strange, he thought as he turned away from her to inspect some papers on his desk. His first baptised had committed murder, his second baptised had thieved, his third had committed adultery, and yet he loved them so much that the pain in his heart felt as if he was close to dying. 'Are you going to be married?' he whispered.

'I don't know, Father. He's divorced.'

'Is he a Catholic?

'Yes, Father, but his wife is a Protestant and they were married in a registry office.'

He tried to sound angry. 'Stella,' he said sternly, 'what was the purpose of your confession? Were you truly repentant? I'm talking now as your priest.'

Her bottom lip quivered and tears filled her eyes. 'I wanted you to understand, Father. That's what you said you wanted, the understanding of why the murders happened. But of course I'm sorry too, sorry I had to kill. I never wanted to kill anyone. In a perfect world I would never have feared about going straight to the authorities. But it's not a perfect world, far from it. It's corrupt. How long do you think I could have stayed alive as a witness against the drugs people? I was given information recently that my instincts had been correct. Charles would probably have got away with the murders. I was told his sister-in-law had voiced her suspicions about her husband's death after Charles had rowed with him over something to do with the fishing fleet. Later, she retracted her statement, and then moved away from the area. Father, it is possible that he murdered, or had killed, his own brother. What chance did I have against such a ruthless man?

'Oh, Father, of course I want absolution for my soul. Believe me, Father, the guilt from that act of murder really haunts me. It's horrible to live with that guilt. So I can justify the terrible act, I have to think of my actions as part of a holy war against an evil. Father, I have the right to save my life, the right to try to prevent myself from going into prison. I have the right to save myself from what would have been a moral injustice. If the way I have chosen seems devious, then all I can say is you should hear some of the lies that are told in a court of law, under oath.

'Believe me, Father, just because I don't want to go to prison doesn't mean I'm not truly repentant of a mortal sin.'

176

Her jaw was clenched defiantly, her eyes reproachful. She looked just as she had when she was eight years old, and he had ticked her off for hitting a boy in the playground. 'Little girls can't go round punching boys in the face,' he had said to her. To which she had replied, 'Yes they can, Father, if the boys are bullies.'

He took hold of her and hugged her. She clung to him.

'You are my first baptised one Stella, and I love you dearly. You are like my own child. I loved your father, your mother – and your brother, too, is a wonderful young boy with a good soul. I am your friend as well as your priest. And, as your friend, I will always be there.'

While she clung to him he managed to brush away his own tears, and said, 'Now Stella, as my friend, I need help. Could you please do an old priest a favour?'

'I will do anything for you, Father, but give myself up to the police,' she replied.

'Could you spare a day to drive me somewhere? I've asked Jack far too often; I can't ask him again.'

She looked at him with relief. 'Sure, whenever you like,'

'It is a journey I must make,' he said. 'Do you have a tape player thing in your car that works?'

'A cassette player, yes.'

He watched her walk across the road to the Saab. To try to understand the complications of another's mind, to think that he could even lift the corner of the cross, borne by another's life, was such arrogance. The pain was too great for him. Perhaps that was the answer to his prayer, that he could be the channel, if in a state of humility, between one soul repenting and the Boss, but he could never understand.

It was like a peasant planting lettuces, praying to understand the great workings of the inner core of earth, merely from a lifetime's observation of growing lettuces. So many

177

of his assumptions had been wrong, so many of his attempts to follow the labyrinth of life had led him back to where he had started the journey. The quest to find the truth of the Filofax had taught him that only by following the Boss, by waiting patiently for revelation, and in faith, offering his unquestioning service, could he be a true priest after the order of Melchizedek. He had to keep trying to pick up the cross, trying to help, even though he failed time and time again. He must keep trying until his last breath.

Stella had thought she was the last one of her family – he *knew* he was the last one living of his own. His brother, father and mother had died over twenty years ago. Now the Boss had finished with his services in England and arranged to send him to Spain. He decided he must lose his fear of change and accept the favour of warmer weather. He must lose his prejudice about living with a lot of other old priests. Perhaps in old age they needed to serve each other.

'Do you want to talk, or do you want some quiet, Father?'

It was a warm morning, in early May, and Stella had collected him at six-thirty, and brought a hamper with coffee and sandwiches for the journey.

He had given her the tapes he wanted to hear as they drove along.

'I have to make a pilgrimage, Stella,' he said, 'to do penance for an old sin. I would very much like to listen to the tape and be silent.'

'That's fine by me.'

She put on the cassette of the Rosary, Celebrant His Holiness the Pope John Paul II. Father Peter sat holding his rosary and listening to *Canto Inicial*. Out of the corner of his eye he could see Stella silently mouthing the words.

She was a good driver, he thought. Her concentration was excellent and he felt absolutely safe in her hands. As the first of the Joyful Mysteries, *The Annunciation*, began, he stopped the tape interrupting the reverent silence with, 'When am I going to meet this policeman you're in love with?'

'We've just heard that he might be transferred to the National Intelligence Criminal Service in Lyons – a sort of Scotland Yard part of Interpol,' Stella replied.

'Well, if you're in Warsaw and he's in Lyons, you're not going to see much of each other,' Father Peter said.

After another long silence he added, 'Perhaps you should both take your holidays at the same time and come to Marbella. Then he could do the decent thing and marry you. You'd better hurry up if you want children.' Stella pressed the tape back into the machine.

As they crossed into the county of Norfolk, he could see that the May flowers were out. Blossoming trees filled the countryside with gentle daubs of pastel colours. Lost childhood memories and emotions were awakened by every village, hamlet and changing landscape. His heart pounded. It seemed as if he could breathe in the past and make a pilgrimage through every precious moment of his life.

They picnicked where they could see buttercups, daisies, dandelions and bluebells scattered across the fields. They saw cows chewing their cud in the shade of old trees, while rooks circled their nests, which resembled large smudges of grey against the trees. Sparrows, wrens and finches darted in and out of the tangled hedgerows.

The music of the first of the Sorrowful Mysteries, the *Agony in the Garden*, filled the car. They drove on, past hills covered by a haze of blue, the imminent efflorescence of lavender. He thought of lavender bags, soft pieces of material stuffed with the fragrant seeds, and remembered her filling them so carefully, placing them into drawers of linen sheets. He felt his eyes swimming. How could she have changed so? How could Old Nick have changed such a beautiful woman?

They arrived at Old Hunstanton just after two o'clock in the afternoon. They drove down an unadopted road towards a hotel close to the track that led to the beach.

'Will you be all right, Father?' Stella asked him as he left her drinking tea in the hotel lounge.

'I shall be at least an hour,' he replied.

The tide was out, the waves were thin threads on the horizon. He could not remember it being difficult to walk along the beach. When he was a boy he would run along the seashore, skimming the ground as a thrown flat pebble flies across the water. Now it took effort to lift one foot in front of the other. His knees cracked as they pulled against the soft, deep, dry sand.

He had to do it, had to make it to the right place. His lungs heaved, his body was perspiring, and he did not know whether it was the sound of the sea or his heart that made the rhythmic pounding noise inside his head. He paused despondently. He was already tired, almost exhausted, from only half a mile's walk, and he wondered whether he should continue on what now seemed a futile gesture.

From a beach hut came a clattering sound. An old woman was placing a kettle on a primus stove. He saw her carefully light a match. Like the old woman lighting the candle and scaring Old Nick from the Dyke, he thought. It was Old Nick who was telling him he was too tired. Old Nick hated anyone to make any effort about anything, except mischief and evil. He pressed on, moving his shoulders, pushing the life back into his legs. The perspiration was running into his eyes, blurring his vision.

And then he heard the shouts. Wiping his eyes he looked ahead and he could see him, the 'little black sheep'. He was hurling abuse at the sky in anger and rage. He was screaming at God. Father Peter kept walking until he could see him clearly. He had been a prisoner here for fifty-eight years, this screaming child.

He drew closer. The boy's face was red and twisted. 'You bloody, bloody God, I hate you. You nasty, stinky, horrible God, I'll kill you, I'll get something dreadful and kill you. You took my mother, you killed my mother, I hate you. I'll never ever pray again. I'll put other gods in front of you, I shan't keep holy the sabbath day, I shall break all your commandments, because I hate you.'

The wailing, screaming rage was terrible. It echoed through Father Peter's soul.

'Bless me, Father, for I have sinned,' he sobbed. 'It is a lifetime since my proper confession. I have sinned against you.'

The child was lying on the beach crying pitifully. Father Peter walked towards him and called his name. The child turned his head and the old priest felt he was drowning in the eyes of the child's anguished soul.

Anger, misplaced anger. Despair. The little black sheep. What could he give this child? A mother's love? Every feminine cell in his body poured out love. He prayed that the Holy Queen would help this child's sorrow, give him salvation.

The child had stopped crying and was looking thoughtfully at him. He kissed his young head with his spirit and dried his sad wet eyes with his breath. Then he offered the child his hand, and was rewarded with a smile.

It was the smile of innocence, faith and hope. A child loved, confident through the charity of spirit. He felt the small hand in his own. Was it his imagination or did the sand feel easier to walk upon?

They talked, he and the child, talked about truth, life and the lies that men tell. And the child gave him the present of understanding – it was trust.

181

He walked the child back along another unadopted road filled with potholes, back to the house where he was born. Father Peter stood looking at his old home. It was time to say goodbye.

He opened the gate and the child ran happily towards the back door. He paused, then turned back to the old priest and smiled. It was the smile of hope and faith. Father Peter blessed him before he disappeared inside the house.

As he walked back to collect Stella, the sky appeared to be brighter, colours were more intense, the air smelled fresher, the sounds of life were clear. And he had lost his tiredness.

'Does it seem a bit brighter to you Stella?' he asked as they drove home.

'It's the light of Easter dispelling the darkness, Father,' she said.